By Aaron Marc Stein

A BODY FOR
A BUDDY

A BODY FOR
A BUDDY

AARON MARC STEIN

PUBLISHED FOR THE CRIME CLUB BY
DOUBLEDAY & COMPANY, INC.
GARDEN CITY, NEW YORK
1981

*All of the characters in this book
are fictitious, and any resemblance
to actual persons, living or dead,
is purely coincidental.*

Library of Congress Cataloging in Publication Data
Stein, Aaron Marc, 1906–
A body for a buddy.
I. Title.
PS3537.T3184B6   813'.52
ISBN 0-385-17583-3
Library of Congress Catalog Card Number 80-2897

For
Christianna Brand
in admiration.

For
Mary and Roland Lewis
with love.

A BODY FOR
A BUDDY

CHAPTER 1

When Thurber said of the woman who went to the Virgin Islands for her divorce that she had always wanted to live in the past, he might have been saying it for me; but any fool should know it doesn't work. It just can't work. A Virgin Islands divorce could relieve her of a husband. It couldn't reflower her.

So why would a guy who knows all that want after twenty years to go back to his college reunion? Was it a middle-aged wish to be a sophomore again? I hope it wasn't that. I like to think I was only trying to update the past. Since for me, after all, the twenty years had been a period of almost nonstop mobility, I had been out of touch.

I am Matt Erridge, and what I do is engineering. More than that, the jobs I get tend to take me to one part or another of the far side of nowhere. They also keep me out there for extended periods of time with never a chance of running into any old buddies. Most of the other guys—the ones who had grown up to be bankers, brokers, business tycoons, college professors, architects, doctors, or lawyers—had been spending the twenty years in places where people are. Even the few who after grabbing the sheepskin had never gone back had had occasions for meeting up with one or another of the old bunch. Closer still were those who had married each other's sisters and even those who had swapped wives. Only a few of us were making the long jump backward, doing the twenty years in a single take.

It was back to the old campus and back to sleeping in a dorm. The married guys—and most of them were married, some even for the second or third time—brought their wives. That produced culture shock, even though the old place wasn't what it had been. The times had changed and it had changed with the times. In our day it had been all male. Let's say it had been monastic without being celibate. Now it's coeducational.

Out of regard for our presumed prejudice in favor of our outmoded way of life, they had provided us with facilities segregated by gender. For shower-room and john there was a Ladies' at one end of each corridor and a Men's at the other. Ladies who had not for twenty years, if ever, walked the length of a public corridor to reach the nearest setup of plumber's porcelain ran the full expressive gamut from giggling blush to outraged wail.

They soon discovered, however, that the long walk was the least of it. Not all of the undergraduates had gone home for the summer. Some were still in residence, and they were having no truck with the inhibitions of their elders. They used what was nearest to hand.

Although we had frequent encounters with coeds in the Men's, I heard no complaints from the good old boys. Wives who had taken the prescribed direction in quest of a shower only to come on 260 pounds of offensive line-backer, who offered them a warm welcome as the water sluiced over his monumental nakedness, told all and sundry that the linebacker was offensive out of the stadium as well as in. Maybe some of them really did mind it, I don't know.

I have no wife, and, since all rooms were doubles, they

had put me in with another bachelor. That was great because the guy was Larry Dawson. Way back then Larry and I had been roommates. That had been taken into consideration by the people who made the arrangements.

It does sound like living in the past, doesn't it? Obviously it could have been except that neither of us was the type for it. We had been friends, at least as close as brothers, and we were still friends, albeit by remote control. For twenty years it had been the annual exchange of Christmas cards and an all too occasional long-distance phone call.

Larry had gone on to med school and had followed it with a life of busy practice and research. All of this he had been doing in a Midwestern city that was nowhere near the places I'd ever been. So Larry was one of my major reasons for going back. Another was Bob Carey. He had been the other roommate, but he was back with his wife. I had never met her, but I knew at first sight that our Bobbie had done all right. She was a funny little woman with a funny face. Her name was Mary, but she would have none of it.

"You call me Slammer," she said. "That's what Bob calls me."

"Why Slammer?"

"Because Mary Carey is impossible. Not quite as bad, perhaps, as Harry Carey, but still impossible. It almost kept me from marrying him but calling me Slammer made it all right."

I can concede that some change might have been required, but I still don't know why Bob settled for "Slammer." Since it was Bob, however, I wasn't surprised. He always had his own names for people, and more often than not the derivations were obscure. Back when I was doing engineering and Larry was pre-med, Bob had been a classics scholar. He'd gone on to run the Ph.D. route and had become a distinguished professor of Greek. It's likely that by one of Bob's convoluted processes "Slammer" had a Greek origin.

Seen over the distance of the twenty years, such spaces as there might have been between us in undergraduate days were now looking much smaller than they had been. Even guys who in those days had been anything but friends were buddying up as though on their last encounter they hadn't been trying to kill each other.

I'm not exaggerating. There was Ham Roberts. Probably because he was someone I hadn't wanted to remember, I had forgotten Hamilton Roberts. I've had friends and I've had enemies, but there haven't been many people I can say I have hated. Hamilton Roberts, though, I did hate. I guess it had been simmering between the two of us for most of the four years. Then one night not long before graduation the thing had exploded. It was a fight, savagely bloody, no holds barred.

The guy owed it to Larry and Bob that he had survived that night. They pulled me off him and they wrestled me down long enough for him to crawl away out of reach. I had been well on the way to killing him and determined to take it all the way.

As soon as I saw him, I remembered, and I told myself that this was one guy I'd be giving a wide berth. Certainly there was nothing there anyone could want to revive. He had changed, but not too much. He had put on a little fat and a lot of gloss. He had his wife with him and she had him outglossed.

Bob was the first to spot her.

"That," he said, "is for the geologists."

"If this doesn't go down in history as the robbery reun-

ion," Slammer said, "it will only be because the underworld isn't what it's cracked up to be."

It was the babe's jewelry. You could have charged admission and set her up as a rival attraction to that room in the
Tower of London where tourists go to gawk at the crown
jewels. Okay, she wasn't wearing the Black Prince's ruby,
but she was hung all over with diamonds and emeralds. To
borrow a word from the olive bottles, there wasn't a rock
on her that wouldn't grade as super-colossal.

She drew every eye. I had picked up enough on the old
crowd to know that there were no few financial heavy-
weights among them, but all the other wives had held it
down to nothing more than the engagement ring and wedding band plus maybe a string of pearls or a gold chain. In
that company Mrs. Hamilton Roberts was a showstopper.

I hadn't wanted it to be that way, but I was caught looking. Her husband's eye met mine. His pudgy face split into
the world's happiest grin. He waved.

So what? It had all been a long time ago. Why can't
bygones be bygones to the extent of brewing up some kind
of a smile and returning the bastard's wave? If he isn't
holding grudges, how can you, Matt Erridge? After all,
you're the one who was on top in that fight. Why I should
have thought that it could stop there I'll never know. It
didn't.

He broke his Christmas tree away from some people she
had been chatting up and propelled her across the green
straight at us. Let's be specific: it was straight at me. He
came on in a big way. It wasn't just the heavy handshake
or the friendly slap on the back. It was the full treatment, a
crushing bear hug and a rapid pounding behind the shoulder. If you've been down in Latin America, you should
know it. They call it the *abrazo* and it's their standard well-

met-old-buddy routine. Along with it he was roaring with uncontrollable joy.

"Matt Erridge," he shouted. "Matt, you old bastard. Twenty years! How've you been?"

I played the game. I swapped my "old bastard" for his. I hugged and I pounded. I couldn't believe that he had forgotten or that, at least on sight of me, recollection would not have come flooding back, but evidently bygones were to be bygones. You don't go to reunions to revive old feuds. I had no expectation that at long last I was going to find myself liking the guy, but he was the one who could have been feeling that he had a grudge to hold. If he wasn't holding one, how could I?

Backing away from it, he handed Larry and Bob greetings a touch less vociferous. Bob introduced him to Slammer. With her, Ham put on a performance that began to fill me in on some of the reasons I had never liked him. It was unctuous. It was exaggerated. It had such overdone courtliness as hadn't been seen since the storming of the Bastille knocked off that kind of *ancien régime* hogwash.

Slammer took it with a twinkle. She was too kind to laugh in the idiot's face, but keeping it bottled up was costing her an effort. The walking treasury stood by, waiting for him to remember she was there. The situation called for something: I didn't know how long she could be expected to stand there just glittering. There was the wedding band, a diamond-studded circlet on the suitable finger. You had to be looking for it, overwhelmed as it was by that multitude of gigantic brethren, but I spotted it. I introduced myself.

"Mrs. Roberts," I said, "I am Matt Erridge."

"Hello, Matt," she said. "Call me glad."

I took that for a new twist on "glad to meet you." Since her husband was still going through all those flourishes with Slammer, I presented Larry and Bob. Each time she came up with the same response.

"Hello, Larry. Call me glad."

"Hello, Bob. Call me glad."

By the time we had been through all that, Roberts woke up. He introduced Slammer to her.

"Mary," he said. "My wife, Gladys."

That straightened me around. I did the quick revision to give her the upper-case G.

"Hello, Gladys."

That set the two women off.

"Call me Glad, Mary."

"Call me Slammer, Glad."

Roberts broke in on it. Flinging an arm around me, he all but shoved me into his wife.

"This bastard, Matt," he said, "he's special. This is a guy I want you to know. Last time we were together, we had a fight and, baby, was that a fight!" He turned to me. "Remember, Matt?" he asked.

I wasn't going to tell him what I remembered, particularly not in front of his wife.

"It was a long time ago," I said.

"It seems like yesterday," he said.

Bob took a hand.

"That," he said, "would have to be because you've been having an empty life. It should seem like twenty years ago."

"Empty life?" Roberts said. "Yes, empty of fights like that. Bastards like good old Matt you don't run onto every day. Otherwise it's been full enough."

We moved it to a table and talked over drinks. We were

out in the dorm quadrangle. You know the let's-pretend-
we-were-founded-by-a-Plantagenet deal. Everything is gray
and Gothic and everything has a green lawn in its middle.
They had tables dotted all over the grass and a beer bar at
one side and the hard stuff across the way.

It was where have you been these twenty years and what
have you been doing. Larry, Bob, and I knew about each
other. So it was Ham Roberts asking and not listening
much to the answers. The questions were no more than a
necessary prologue to his own recital. We were filled in
thoroughly on where Ham Roberts had been.

His twenty years had been something like mine in that
most of the time had been spent out of the country, but
there the resemblance ended. Where I had made my career
working for the guys who push the millions around, Hamilton Roberts had become one of the heavy-laden. He was in
oil, and that doesn't mean like sardines. His stamping
ground had been Venezuela and he made it abundantly
and repetitively clear, that the *abrazo* habit wasn't the only
thing he'd picked up down there. The heavy encrustation
that adorned his lady appeared to be no more than the tip
of the iceberg. If there wasn't more ice where all that had
come from, he was making no secret of the fact that the
big bucks that can buy such baubles were there. He not
only number-dropped till the table seemed to be littered
with his references to seven figures, he also name-dropped.

It was "Bunker." It was "Nels, may he rest in peace." It
was "John, God rest his soul." He wrapped all those given
names around with more than enough hints to make certain that even the dullest of us would not fail to flesh it out
with Rockefeller, Hunt, and Getty.

About the time he was in midstream we were joined by
the Culver Hoyts, Culver and Florence, and they were al-

most as glossy as Ham and Glad. From the way Florence looked at Glad's array of geologic specimens it took no special mind-reading talent to know that she was hating herself for having left so many of hers in the vault. Culver was a guy I just barely remembered. It was only because of Larry that I remembered him at all. Back in those great, silly days he had been a dim figure.

Like Larry he had been doing pre-med, but unlike Larry, for him it had been tough going. He had to slog away at it if he was going to get by, and there'd been no time for fun and games. We, on the other hand, had been the fun-and-games gang. I spent those years fallen into bad company. Both Larry and Bob were way up there at the genius level. It was no sweat at all for them to grab off honors and that with almost no studying. So could Erridge keep his nose stuck in the books all the time when those two merry apes were cavorting around him?

He couldn't. We played. We sowed the proverbial wild oats, and Erridge managed to get by, but mostly because each time he was about to do the terminal slide down the academic skids, his roommates would take time out from going ape to give him the coaching that would haul him back to safe ground.

I suppose I should have had some fellow feeling for Culver since, for all his slogging, he would never have made it without Larry's help. The only memory of him I could dredge up was of a whining sobersides who would come around to the room to suck Larry into translating organic chemistry into one-syllable words for him. So, when the Hoyts joined us, they were, in fact, joining Larry. Larry was too polite to let it show, but I knew him too well not to get the feeling. It came out of him like the air off a glacier, a just perceptible chill.

They hadn't stayed with us long before they were sloping off, but not to join a crowd at some other table. Wearing the air of a guy who had just remembered an important letter he had to mail, Culver propelled his Florence before him and they left the Quad. It seemed most unlikely that he'd felt the chill. Larry had been doing too good a job of masking it, and I remembered Culver as a thick-skinned dope who never in his life caught a nuance even though in those good old days our nuances had been anything but subtle. It seemed more likely that even a few minutes of the Ham Roberts success story had given him all of that he could ever have wanted, and that even a brief exposure to Glad's blaze of glory had bitten too deeply into his wife's soul.

I'd had more than enough of the monologue, but I had come around to not even half listening. Something too astonishing had turned up at one of the tables across the Quad. A lot of the old classmates had become familiar faces I couldn't quite place, and with some even a hard squint at the name tag was no help. Now, however, I was having a moment of instant recognition.

She hadn't been a classmate. You will remember that we were pre-coeducation, but so far as any female could have been woven into the fabric of our undergraduate life, she had been. She had been part of our education, the cohabitation part. I have no reliable statistics on just how many of us had been welcomed into her bed at one time or another, but the numbers would be greater than you could easily believe.

She had changed, but not much. It seemed to me that she had worn remarkably well, but then she had always been a durable type. I couldn't say that it wasn't peculiarly suitable that she should be a part of our reunion. At the same time, however, it seemed too peculiar. I could hardly believe that she had been provided for the few unwived characters like Larry and myself. It was unlikely that the arrangements committee should have been that thoughtful of us, and certainly the prospect of her rubbing shoulders with their wives might have been expected to give them pause.

I looked at Larry. He was seeing what I saw.

"It is, isn't it?" I said.

"Sooey," Larry said, "and no one else."

Ham turned to look. His florid color went noticeable shades more florid.

"Jesus!" he said.

Then it came back to me. I remembered what it had been that triggered our big fight. We had fought over Sooey. It hadn't been for possession—none of us had been possessive about her. It had only been young Erridge stricken with a knight-in-shining-armor moment. In my own way of being a male chauvinist pig, I had felt that sporting anything like a shiner and a thick lip had to be kept as a masculine prerogative.

At that point Bob caught up with it.

"Damned if it isn't," he said. "Sooey in the flesh, and actually in more abundant flesh."

Slammer jabbed a forefinger into his gut.

"That, my lad," she said, "is a case of the pot calling the kettle round."

"Her name was Amanda," Ham said.

"Was it?" Larry asked. "We had our own name for her."

He gave it in full and Slammer picked it up.

"*Sui generis?*" she asked. "Was she unique back then? She looks about average now."

"Oh," Ham said. "Greek. I never knew any Greek."

"Latin," Bob said.

"Greek, Latin—no difference." Ham Roberts was outraged. "What's she doing here?"

"She's reuning even as you and I," Larry told him. "She's not the only one. All the class widows were invited."

Ham's outrage mounted.

"That isn't funny."

"Of course it isn't," Bob said. "If widowhood isn't a tragic condition, it should be."

"Look, guys," Ham said. "Not in front of the ladies."

"I like things in front of me," Slammer said. "I don't care for them behind my back."

Ham shrugged. "If you like," he said. "But me, I didn't drag Glad here for this." He was on his feet and pulling his dazzling mate out of her chair. "We'll see you later," he said.

He was taking flight, but he had waited too long. Sooey had made a start in our direction. As he moved, she swerved. She had always been fleet of foot, and she was still nimble. Darting for him, she cut him off neatly. He hadn't made it so far that we couldn't hear her greeting and his response.

"Ham Roberts," she said. "It is you, isn't it? I'd have known you anywhere."

He probably wanted to say he wasn't he, but he didn't get to say anything before she was right in there planting the big, juicy kiss on his crimson kisser. He had to wait till he could get out from under that before he could speak.

"This is Amanda," he said. "Mandy, my wife, Gladys."

"Hello, Mandy. Call me Glad." Her formula never failed her.

"Great to see you, Mandy," Ham said. "We've got to run."

"If you've got to run, you've got to run," Sooey said. "See you around."

It had never been for her conversation that we valued Sooey.

"Sure," Ham said, hauling his Gladys away.

It didn't seem to bother Sooey any. She just went back on course, again heading for our table.

"Well and well and well," she said, "if it isn't the Three Mosquitos."

Memories, memories, memories. I had forgotten it had been her name for us, and no more than fair since we'd had ours for her.

She took us one by one.

"Larry—sweet, sweet Larry."

He got one of those kisses, but, as he had always been, he was a better man than Ham Roberts. He responded in kind. Coming away from that, she bounced off to me.

"And Mattie, darling Mattie, and how are all the lovely muscles?"

We kissed. I'm not going to say anything Larry could do I could do better. Anyhow it's no great accomplishment. Anybody can pucker up.

That left Bob, but not for long. She forged right ahead to complete her rounds.

"And Bobbie—Bobbie the Brain. You know, most of what you would say, Bobbie darling, I never understood, but it didn't matter. I could always shut you up."

Bob started to say something, but for Sooey it was just the opportunity for a demonstration.

"Like this," she said. "This is the way I did it."

So Bob got his kiss. Although I'd never thought of him

as a competitive type, that time he went to town. He put both Larry and me to shame. Slammer was loving every moment of it. I've never seen a woman enjoy anything more.

It had to end sometime and in time it did. He came out of it and introduced her to Slammer.

"Slammer," he said, "I want you to know Amanda Graystock. Without her I would not have had my early understanding of Catullus."

"*Da mi basia mille, deinde centum,*" Slammer said.

Bob picked it up.

   "'*Dein mille altera, dein secunda centum*
   Deinde usque altera mille, deinde centum.'"

"Your Greek," Sooey said. "I remember."

"Latin," Bob said.

"Sorry. Latin. It's the one about the hundred kisses and then a thousand and so on and so on."

"The other way around," Bob said. "A thousand and then a hundred."

"A lot anyway." She turned to Slammer. "I heard that he was married, and I thought it had to be a great woman if she caught one of these three devils, and of course you are. You can even talk to him and you can understand what he says."

"Some of the time," Slammer said. "Between the hundred and the thousand."

Sooey sat down with us and I went to the bar to get her a drink. All the while I was mumbling to myself. Bob had called her Amanda Graystock. I was mouthing the name, trying it for sound. Because we'd always had our own name for her—it had been Bob's originally—I hadn't even remembered Amanda, but on hearing it I clicked on that

much of it immediately. Amanda had the right recollecta-
ble ring. Graystock, however, was something else again. I
couldn't make it ring true. What her surname had been I
couldn't remember, but Graystock sounded all wrong.

I brought her the drink and the five of us couldn't have
been more cosy. She stayed with us for the duration of the
drink and then with another round of kisses—this time
there was one for Slammer as well—she moved on. Obviously she was touching all the bases and she had a lot of
bases to touch.

"Fun," Slammer said after she had left us, "but hardly
unique."

"You're spelling her wrong," Bob said. "It's S-o-o-e-y
G-e-n-e-r-o-u-s, the generous pig."

Slammer valiantly suppressed her laugh. She even
worked up a disapproving scowl.

"That was nasty," she said.

"Of course it was nasty," Larry agreed. "We were nasty
little boys."

"And grown up with your nastiness undimmed,"
Slammer said.

"Those," Bob said, "were our salad days. Sooey was the
dressing."

I was thinking the undressing, but I shoved that aside. I
was still trying to make Graystock fit her.

"What's with the Graystock?" I asked. "I can't remember, but I'm sure it wasn't Graystock."

"It wasn't," Larry said. "And damned if I remember
what it was. Anyhow, you've been out of touch. Remember
George Daniel Graystock?"

"Walking skeleton with glasses," Bob said.

"He was always losing them and he walked around
bumping into things."

So that was something else that came back to me.

"G.D.G.," I said. "We called him God-Damn Gruesome. I remember now."

"If you idiots hadn't had all those special names for people," Slammer said, "your lives might have been less complicated."

"That they would, Mary Carey," Bob said. "I'd still be a bachelor."

"Forget I ever spoke," Slammer said.

"Sometime when he was without his glasses," Larry said, "he bumped into the altar and with Sooey. That was about eight years ago."

I had the thought that eight years back she could have reached the place where she would have been a bit too far along for yet another generation of undergraduates or it could have been that she had moved away from it before she could become the victim of coeducation. I kept the thoughts to myself. I'd already heard from Slammer about nastiness.

"Then the class widow touch wasn't a gag?" I said.

"He died this past year," Larry told me. "A quick terminal coronary."

"I thought it was the beefy guys who get the coronaries," I said. "The skeletons live forever because they've never really lived."

"You can't say he never lived," Bob said. "The best part of eight years with Sooey—can you call that not living?"

"The myth has it that it's the women who gossip," Slammer said.

"Not any more," I said. "These days we're all unisex."

Bob changed the subject. He asked Larry the question I'd been meaning to ask.

"What about your old buddy?"

"Which old buddy? You or Matt?"

"Dr. Culver Hoyt, MD?"

Larry winced.

"Dr. Culver Hoyt, MD," he said. "MD for more dung. You remember the way he was. Pathetically stupid."

Larry gave us the rundown on Culver Hoyt. The way he put it, you didn't have to be stupid to be a surgeon. There were plenty of brainy ones, but there were also no few surgeons who were doing very well for themselves and even sometimes for their patients without a brain in their heads.

"That's why it's smart to have a second opinion before you let one of those babies get you on the table," Larry said. "The operating process is largely a manual thing. A guy who's good with his hands has much of what it takes. It's like being a plumber or an electrician. Arrant dopes will do the most delicate and complicated things with wires or pipes and they don't need to have the first understanding of what they are doing. It may not be exactly like that, but it comes close enough. It's on the diagnostic part that the stupid ones fall down. It's like the dumb and greedy garage man who tells you you'll need a dozen new parts when all that's wrong is the points need cleaning."

"What kind of surgery does he do?" Slammer asked.

"You keep away from him," Larry told her. "He's gynecological. He snaps out a uterus at the drop of a fee. You won't find a guy anywhere who does a neater unnecessary operation. I blame myself. If I hadn't dragged him through organic chemistry by the seat of his pants, he would never have made it into med school. That would have been a great service to womankind."

"From the look of them, it's been many a uterus and many a fee," I said.

"Too many," Larry said, "and only the most expensive

ones. Our man Culver is a fashionable surgeon. The Hoyts move in the circles where the money is. Call-me-Glad could be a typical Culver Hoyt patient."

"How did he get to be so fashionable?" Bob asked.

"The time-tested way. He married the boss's debutante daughter. He went into practice with his father-in-law, high society's pet obstetrician, rich as Croesus and famous for timing labor to the social schedule, both the patient's and his own. All the tricks for bringing labor on or holding it off. Nobody ever missed a party. The guy was a master of timing in every respect. He stayed around till he had son-in-law established and, when Culver was ready to inherit, daddy-in-law obligingly dropped dead."

Slammer was beginning to look thoughtful.

"I'm wondering," she said. "Outside of you three, was there anyone here who wasn't an abysmal schmuck?"

We assured her that the old class was heavy with great guys—none, of course, as great as ourselves, but she wasn't to expect that much. We pulled away from our table and mingled with the mob. It was all right. The good guys were still good guys and plenty of those I'd thought were pretty dim surprised me. It might have been that they'd improved with age. Better to think that than to believe that I had mellowed.

There was dinner and there was dancing. Undergraduate singing groups sang for us and with us. Bob and Larry and I would have sunk without a trace when it came to the words of the football fight songs if it hadn't been for Slammer. When we broke down, she fed the lyrics to us. I guessed it was because she would have been up in the stands singing while the three of us had been down on the field knocking heads with nothing like a song on our lips.

I was thinking that she would have been going with

someone else back in those days because, if it had been Bob, I would have known her then. When I asked her, she told me that she had learned the songs in her cradle. Her father and a flock of uncles taught them to her.

"When you heroes were giving your all for the honor of the school," she said, "I was in the stands with daddy, complete in my Mary Janes and with braces on my teeth. In those days Mary Janes were shoes, not grass."

"Then you're just a baby."

"Five years younger than Bob," she said. "When it's the five between thirteen and eighteen, it's a generation gap."

CHAPTER 2

When Slammer and Bob called it bedtime, we broke it up. The we was just our own little quartet. A dance floor had been set up under a tent at one side of the Quad, and a horde of the old gang were jumping up and down. They were showing every sign of going on forever. Our rooms overlooked the Quad. I suppose this Gothic cloister architectural style worked well for the cloistered, particularly well for such as may have taken a vow of silence.

You could, however, go through the whole roster of old buddies and their mates and you wouldn't ever come up with any vows of silence. Furthermore there was a rock band. Wall all that in on the four sides with battlemented stone facades, and you have eardrum-shattering time. We told the Careys that they were out of their skulls. Didn't they recognize that they had fallen into a nest of sleep-murderers?

"Slammer, my love," I said, "you won't even be able to hear Bob snore."

"He doesn't snore and, in case you haven't heard, Matthew, my love, for the happily married bed and sleep are not necessarily synonymous."

With that they left us and all of a sudden Larry and I found ourselves at loose ends. Neither of us had any inclination toward cutting in on the dancing and no greater inclination toward joining any of the groups that had settled in for serious drinking. We pulled out of the Quad and toured the campus, dropping in on a few other classes at their reunions. We wandered around, checking them out. It was ten minutes here and a quarter of an hour there and intervals in between when it was just the two of us alone drifting from one headquarters to the next.

Somewhere along the line we were separated for an hour or thereabouts. Larry got involved with some guys he had known professionally and I got caught up with some fellow engineers. About the time that things began to die we joined up again. It seemed to us that we were hitting the hour when we could go back to our own place and catch some sleep. If guys who were only fifteen years out were packing it in, the lads in our age bracket should also have been folding.

The very young classes—the one-to-fives—were still going strong. They would be up and roaring all through the night, but we were well past wanting to go playing around with kids who would look up from their crap games long enough to call us "sir." Perhaps we hadn't come back with the thought of being young again; certainly we hadn't come back to be made to feel our age.

We wandered back to our Quad and, as we had expected, the rock band had finished its gig and had been paid off. The Quad wasn't totally deserted. There were still a few people talking at a few of the tables, but they were keeping it down. It may have been out of regard for a few others who hadn't been up to making it to bed and were slumped on the tables, heads buried in arms and slumbering peacefully.

We headed up to our room. Those dorm corridors are dimly lit, but there was light enough for us to see the kid. As soon as we came to the top of the stairs, we saw him, or at least that part of him that he had positioned for inspection—his butt. Since he was bent over, he was putting conspicuous strain on the seat of his jeans. He was bent over with an easily recognizable purpose.

The guy was down there with his eye to the keyhole of our room. Larry and I stopped. We looked at it. We looked at each other. We said nothing. We didn't need to. We had lived together those four years and even these many years later the lines of silent communication were still open and still functioning perfectly.

Larry dipped in his pocket and came up with the quarter. I pointed at the seat of his pants. He pointed at my head. I was taking tails. He was taking heads. He flipped the coin. It came up heads and I swallowed my disappointment. I stood back while Larry crept up behind the peeper. With perfect aim and nicely calculated force he planted his kick. The kid's head banged against the door, damaging neither since he had more than enough hair to cushion it. He also had quick reflexes. He didn't even look around to see what hit him. He took off in a quick scuttle for the stairs. I let him brush past me, holding back on my kick until he would be where he needed it most. I let go on it just in time to help him down the stairs.

Larry and I met at the door to our room. We stood together for a moment and shook hands. I suppose that was living in the past. The twenty years were but a moment gone.

We opened the door and went in. We didn't have to unlock it. That's part of dormitory life. People rarely lock doors. We stood a moment in the doorway, startled and just a touch confused. I know what I was thinking and it seemed obvious that Larry would be sharing the thought. We had expected to come into a dark room. The place had been full of afternoon sun when we had last been up there. We could have had no reason then to have turned on the desk lamp. So it couldn't have been that we had turned it on and neglected to switch it off. Also one of our two beds was occupied and the occupant was a female. From where we stood we could make out no more than the general shape of her, but there could be no question but that it was a her.

We backed out of there together. It had to be that we were confused and had barged into the wrong room. Out in the corridor we checked the room number stenciled on the door. It was the number we both remembered. Not trusting our memories, we hauled out of our pockets the instruction sheets they'd given us on checking in. Those instructions told you everything you had to know—what was happening and where and when. Among other things your sheet told you the number of the room to which you had been assigned. We hadn't gone wrong. It was our visitor who had picked the wrong door.

"Do we just go away and let her sleep it off?" Larry asked.

"There's a husband somewhere who'll be looking for her," I said. "He'll be looking unless he's too passed out to know she's strayed."

"Or unless she's one of the widows," Larry said. "No husband extant."

"Let's see if she's anyone we know," I said.

"What difference will that make?"

I couldn't see that it made any difference. I didn't stop to think of why it might have seemed to me that it could.

"I'm going to wake her," I said.

"No," Larry said. "I'll do it. It's more in my field than in yours."

We went back in. I turned the desk lamp so its light fell on the bed. It was Sooey, and she looked terrible. Larry bent over her. She was on the bed I had expected to use, and the light I had turned that way fell on my suitcase. It was standing beside the bed and I was certain that was not where I had left it. There was also something else about it that was not the way I'd left it. The lock hasps were standing straight up, not down flat as they should have been.

I all but forgot about Sooey while my mind filled up with questions about the suitcase. It wasn't as though I had anything so much or anything so important in it— razor, toothbrush, a few changes of clothes, and that was about all of it. So I wasn't worrying about theft. A shirt? A pair of socks? I could think of nothing I'd packed that couldn't easily be replaced in a morning trip into the university store. It was just that upsetting feeling of privacy invaded. If you've ever been the victim of a burglary, you should know what I mean.

If it hadn't been for the suitcase diversion, I would probably have been quicker to wonder at what Larry was doing. Whether gentle or brutal, there are the standard approaches to waking a sleeping woman or rousing a drunken one. You talk to her. You take her by the shoulder and shake her a little. Your may even shake her a lot. You soak a washcloth in cold water and sponge her face with it. You dribble a little ice water on her neck. You might even take a whole glassful and dash it into her face.

It dawned on me that Larry was doing none of these things. I left the suitcase for thinking about later and joined him by the bed. He was drawing back one of her eyelids.

"That passed out?" I asked.

"She's dead."

I don't remember what I said. It must have been at least blasphemous. I do remember that I went on to ask if there wasn't something that could be done. I suppose I was thinking something like artificial respiration or some medical thing like a shot of adrenalin to the heart. I guess I've picked up some notions along those lines from the couple of times I've fallen into a hospital drama on the tube while waiting for the ball game to come on.

"Nothing," Larry said. "She's been gone for some time. It could even be as much as an hour. If anything can be done, it must be done within seconds."

He had gone over to the desk and had picked up the phone. He was dialing the operator.

"Heart?" I asked.

"No telling without an autopsy."

"I suppose she got to feeling ill and went looking for some place she could lie down till she felt better. An empty room . . ."

I didn't go on with it. Larry had the operator. He was asking for the hospital.

"Why the hospital?" I asked while he was waiting to be put through. "If there's nothing that can be done."

"Nothing like that, but the official formalities. A local man should be handling those. Since she died on campus, I'm thinking someone from the university infirmary."

He got through and identified himself. They put him on to one of the university physicians. At that point he went into medical language and I stopped listening. My mind went back to the suitcase. I was thinking that, even if something had been swiped out of it, it had never been of any great importance and now it would certainly be even less so. The next thought, of course, reared up and contradicted what had been going through my mind previously.

Here was something that just didn't fit. There was no way I could look at it to make it fit. She was feeling ill. She went looking for a bed she could flop into till she would be feeling better. She didn't feel better. She died on the bed. So why would she have gone into my suitcase? For what? Also when?

Could she have been hoping to find something she could take to make her feel better? There are those things they advertise for acid indigestion. It seemed crazy, but I was telling myself that maybe at point of death people don't always make the best of sense.

I squatted down by the suitcase and opened it. Don't ask me what I was looking for. It couldn't have been the patent medicine junk she hadn't found because it had never been there. Checking the thing over took only a matter of moments. I hadn't packed so much that I couldn't see all of it pretty well at a glance.

As soon as I'd lifted the lid, even at that one glance, I saw something I hadn't packed. More than that, it was something I had never even owned. It was a small, squat bottle of brown glass and it had a couple of capsules in it. I was just staying there hunkered down with the thing in my hand, trying to figure it.

Finished at the phone, Larry came up behind me and took it out of my hand.

"You take this stuff?" he asked.

He'd opened the bottle and was holding the capsules spilled out on the flat of his hand.

"Those? No, I don't take anything."

"Then what the hell do you carry them around for?"

"I don't. They're not mine."

"It's your suitcase, Matt."

"I know it's my suitcase. I just found them here in my

suitcase, but they're not mine. I've never seen them before. When we came in here just now, I noticed that the suitcase was here by the bed and that's not where I left it. I also noticed that the lock hasps were up and that wasn't the way I left them."

"You left your case locked?"

"No, not locked. You didn't leave yours locked either, did you? But I left mine with the lock hasps down flat." I looked over at his case. "Like yours are," I said. Even while I was talking, I was coming down with the notion that I had revelations. Everything seemed to be coming clear for me. "The poor, silly bitch," I said.

"Never mind that," Larry said. "These things worry me."

He was, of course, talking about the capsules.

"I know what she did," I said. "Crazy, of course, but you know what she was like. She was feeling ill. She went looking for a place where she could lie down. She found our room empty. Then she thought the pain had to be her stomach. People do make that mistake, don't they? She got the idea of looking for something she could take. She found those in your bag and she took the bottle out, putting your bag back the way she found it. She took one of those and tried to put the remaining ones back in your bag. By that time she was too bad off to get anything right. She made the mistake of putting them in my bag instead and by then she was past doing anything like putting my bag back the way she'd found it. It has to be that way. There's no other possibility, Larry."

"Except for two things," Larry said. "First she didn't find anything like this in my bag. I don't carry this stuff around. Second she wasn't looking for something she could take for a pain in her gut and taking just anything she could find. You're thinking a coronary and the mistakes people make in self-diagnosis of heart pain. She didn't die of a coronary, Matt. She died of this stuff."

"You said there was no telling without an autopsy," I reminded him.

"That was before I saw the capsules and the bottle."

"What are the capsules?"

"Phenobarbital."

"Overdose?"

"You can call it that. Standard dosage when taken along with alcohol becomes an overdose. It's a lethal combination."

He had disposed of those revelations I'd been having, but they were immediately replaced with what seemed to me to˙ be fresh revelations.

"Sooey, poor idiot," I said. "I can just see what she did."

"Can you?"

"Yes. She'd had too much to drink. She's feeling lousy. She goes looking for a place where she can lie down."

"You've been through all that."

"Yes, but here's where it gets to be different. She lies down in here but that doesn't help much. She's in something like the world-whirling-around stage. She has those things for sleeping and she carries them with her in her purse. So she comes down with the idiot idea of taking some and going to sleep."

"Then how come they end up in your suitcase?" Larry asked.

"She's totally muddled," I said. "She thinks she's putting them back into her purse. She's reached the place where she doesn't know a suitcase from a handbag."

I had launched into that in full confidence, but even while I was putting it into words, that fine confidence was

ebbing. I couldn't see any kind of purse or handbag anywhere, and I was beginning to remember something else.
What about the kid we had caught at the keyhole? What
had he seen? What more had he been hoping to see?

All the time I was talking there was no change in Larry's
look of worried skepticism. He waited till I'd finished before he spoke.

"She carries those around with her," he said, talking
more to himself than to me. "There are people who do,
people who take them as though they were after-dinner
mints. There are women who will take them out of the
pharmacist's bottle and put them into a pretty little pill
box—gold, silver, tortoiseshell, something like that. She carried hers around in the pharmacy bottle but with the pre-
scription label ripped off it?"

"That kid," I said. "We should have grabbed him."

Larry groaned.

"Will you know him if you see him again?"

"I doubt it." I was groaning with him. "A lot of hair and
blue jeans. On campus these days there'll be too many of
them like that. Did you get a better look?"

"I got a great look at the seat of his pants," Larry said.
"Think I'm going to spot him just on ass recognition?"

I started out of the room. "He may still be hanging
around," I said.

"You think so after the send-off we gave him?"

"Probably not, but I'll try. There are other keyholes."

I didn't have all that much confidence in it, but I was
stuck with a compulsion to go looking for the kid. From
that best of all viewpoints, hindsight, I could see all too
clearly that the two of us had muffed it. I wasn't blaming
Larry. I was blaming myself. He had done his part properly. A boot in the ass had been no more than the young

twerp had coming to him. Teaching him manners and possibly even morals was a suitably adult thing to have done.

It was Erridge who had pulled the rock. Instead of giving him that assist down the stairs—he could have made the stairs quite well enough on his own—I should have grabbed him and held him. If we couldn't have had out of him what he had been watching and what he had seen, we should have turned him over to the campus cops. There are deans and people like that. It is their job to deal with the errant student.

I had taken the law into my own hands. All right, it was my own foot, but I should have known better.

He was nowhere along the corridor. I hadn't expected he would be. They don't come that incorrigible. I went down into the Quad. It was deserted. Even the guys who had been folded over the tables asleep were now gone from there. Good buddies had dragged them indoors and dumped them into bed. I had only one more idea left to me. Mightn't a kid who peeped through one keyhole be hooked on keyholes?

He hadn't been up in our corridor, but there were all the other entries and all the other corridors. I went obsessive on it, trying entry after entry, prowling all the corridors. Now and again I came on a sleepy classmate headed for a john to unload some excess of the beer cargo he had taken on, but there was never a keyhole anywhere that had an eye at it and nowhere did I come on anything young and shaggy. After doing the round of the dorm, I had come full circle and I was back at our entry. I returned to the room. It was now jammed with people—the doctor from the infirmary, a dean, campus cops, and town cops.

Larry was giving them the complete account of everything we knew. At least it was almost complete. The dead

woman was Amanda Graystock, widow of our late classmate, George D. Graystock. He omitted any mention of
her Sooey Generous career. *De mortuis nil nisi bonum.* It
wasn't for nothing that I'd roomed with Bob Carey. It
could have been said that in her Sooey manifestation she
had long been dead, but in any case Sooey Generous was
now certainly dead along with Amanda Graystock. Of the
dead you say nothing but good. So had the old-time generosity been good or bad? It's a question that can be left to
the moralists, and one of those I am not. In any case I
didn't think that Larry was leaving out anything material.

There was, however, one other point on which he was
being something less than complete. Although he was explicit about the barbiturate bottle stripped of its label, he
was saying nothing of where I had found it. Picking up
where he had left off, I added that one piece of informa-
tion. Nobody but the dean seemed much interested. The
dean was a guy called Mulligan. Daniel Mulligan.

The doctor who had come over from the infirmary called
him Danny, and I was having some difficulty thinking of
him as a dean. I remembered deans as being elderly types,
loaded with dignity. Here was a dean who was younger
than I was and he looked like a swinger. I had to remind
myself that to the shaggy peeper Dean Danny might well
look venerable and dignified.

"In your bag," he said, "but not yours?"

"Right."

I fed him my theory of how it had come there.

"You left your bag unlocked and you left the room
unlocked?" he asked.

"Here on campus," I said, "we rarely locked anything.
Anyhow, we all knew how to get around locks."

"Times have changed even here on campus," he said.

"People are more mobile than they used to be. All sorts of people come driving into town and particularly at reunion time. The word's gotten around. There's money and there's valuables and all those alumni having too much fun to be bothered with watching anything. Didn't they give you instruction sheets when you checked in?"

"We've got them."

"Haven't you read them?"

"Not studiously."

"On the instruction sheet you are told not to leave your rooms unlocked and not to leave valuables lying about where a sneak thief can get at them. We don't get those things out for our own entertainment."

It was the old, familiar sound. For all his youth and all his swinging looks, he made noises like a dean. It must have been that he felt duty bound to do that much. Once it was done, he made a quick switch out of it. Stern disapproval was replaced by warm solicitude.

"Now you'll be needing beds," he said.

"Hardly enough night left to be worth worrying about," Larry said.

They were in the process of removing Sooey's body.

"We'll be all right here," I said.

It wasn't the thing to say. The words had been spoken out of ignorance. Larry banded together with the doctor out of the infirmary and they set me straight. My bed was going to be out of service. When there has been a death, there must be a change of bed linen before anyone uses the bed again. There were mandatory rites of purification that had to be performed. The mattress and the pillow were to be fumigated.

"But she wasn't in the bed," I said. "Not tucked in

under the sheet or anything like that. She was just stretched out on top of the bedspread."

It made no difference. Come morning, the bed would be removed and replaced with one that carried no possibility of contamination. That, however, would necessarily be waiting till morning. Meanwhile the dean was taking us home with him for what remained of the night. The deanery had a spare bedroom.

Once Dean Danny Mulligan had been metamorphosed from dean to host, he couldn't have been better company. We tip-toed into the house since there was no need to wake his wife and kids. He broke out the whiskey and the three of us had a quiet drink together. Whether he was concerned about the sleep we had lost or about the sleep he himself was losing, he urged us to take our drinks up with us and showed us to our room.

It was only when he left us that I had my first opportunity to ask Larry a question that was bothering me.

"Why weren't you saying anything about the pill bottle having turned up in my suitcase?"

"I didn't find it," Larry said. "You did. Since you wanted to tell them, you told them. It wasn't for me to take it on myself to speak for you."

"Why would I not want it told?"

Larry shrugged.

"Obviously," he said, "no reason. This is going to be a messy business. I couldn't know how much you might want to be involved."

"Not much," I said. "Not any, but she was in our room and the phenobarb bottle was in my bag. Like it or not, I'm that much involved."

"You are. We both are. I just felt that if I said anything about the bottle in your bag, it would be like I was trying to say that this has nothing to do with me, that it was all your baby and I just happened to be there because they had assigned us to room together."

"So what, Larry? Who's going to think she committed suicide over me? Nobody will be flattering me that much. Ladykiller Matt?"

"Except that I can't see it for suicide, Matt," Larry said.

"I know. Accident. She didn't take her life. She just fumbled it away."

"I can't see it for accident either," Larry said. "Sooey was murdered. There's no other possibility."

"Oh, come on, Larry! Who? Why? How?"

He didn't even make a stab at the who or the why. He left it with explaining the how.

"Someone brought her up to the room for a quiet drink, just the two of them together. It was a doctored drink. It was meant to kill her and it did."

"What makes that more reasonable than what we first thought?" I asked. "She was all over the place, having a drink with this one and a drink with that one. It had to add up to more drinks than she could handle. Drunk and sick, she took the capsules, thinking they'd put her to sleep and she'd feel better. She just didn't know what you know about the alcohol and barbiturate combo."

"The bottle with the label stripped off," Larry said. "No reason for stripping it off except making it impossible to trace it. Also she wasn't drinking all that much."

I zeroed in on the first of that. The rest, I thought, was nonsense. I was remembering that she had been touching all bases and that she'd had a lot of bases to touch.

"The label stripped off," I said. "Couldn't it just have fallen off?"

"Druggists glue them on securely. To get it off clean, the

bottle would need to have been emptied and put to soak until the glue loosened. Then it would have been necessary to dry the inside of the bottle thoroughly before returning the capsules to it. I can see no reason why she should have gone to all that bother and actually nobody did go to all that bother. I examined the bottle. The label hadn't been soaked off. It had been scraped off with a knife—a hurry-up job. Bits of the paper are still there glued to the bottle."

So he wasn't just talking off the top of his head. I came around to asking myself if it could be that the rest of what he'd said wasn't the nonsense I'd been thinking it was.

"You said she hadn't been drinking much," I reminded him. "She hoisted one with us and she was all over the place, drinking with this guy and with that guy."

"She was taking drinks with everyone and not drinking much or any with anyone," Larry said. "You didn't notice, but I did. You brought her a drink. She took one small sip out of it if that much. She was working at staying sober. She'd put her drink to her mouth, but the level wouldn't go down. It didn't go down until she had lowered her glass and sneakily tipped some of the whiskey out on the grass. She was real good at it. Nobody noticed."

"How come you noticed?"

"Accident. I just happened to take the wrong moment to move my foot. I got a shoe filled with whiskey. Bob will have the name for it. His old Greeks did it. Pouring libations? Isn't that it?"

"That's it. She was doing it with her whole drink, sip by sip, spill by spill?"

"With most of it. When she moved off from us, she was carrying her glass with her. It was still almost half full and she dumped it on her way to her next port of call. That got me to watching her while she was making the rounds. She was doing it with everyone."

"Then how could she have gotten enough alcohol in her to work with the phenobarb and do her in?" I asked.

"A token sip at each table," Larry said. "The way she was making the rounds, that could have added up to a full drink, though I doubt it. She got it up in the room. She could pour the stuff off on the grass. She couldn't very well pour it on the floor."

"It's crazy," I said.

"I thought it was funny. Now, of course, it's anything but funny."

That he didn't have to spell out for me. Sooey had been up to something. She had been all over the place doing her good old act of the warm-hearted, carefree kid for whom anything goes. She had worked at it and she had done it well. She had been disarming, but she had been set to pull something off and it hadn't worked out. She'd tried it on somebody who was not going to be had. He killed her.

"Murder," I said. "Do you think the kid saw it?"

"He saw something."

"I should have held him. Instead I just helped him on his way. How could I have been that dumb?"

"After the fact?" Larry said. "Anyhow, it doesn't matter. Once the word is out that she's dead, the boy's bound to come forward."

"Think so?"

"Think not?"

"He took off plenty scared," I said. "I'm betting he'll stay scared."

"Scared we'd beat up on him?" Larry asked.

"Could be," I said. "We hadn't made too bad a start.

Also he could be afraid that we'd turn him in. Dean Danny Mulligan might be tough on Peeping Toms."

"Could be," Larry said.

He sounded unconvinced.

We gave up on it and hit our beds. I didn't sleep much. I just tried to hold the tossing and turning down to a decent minimum and all the time I was having the feeling that Larry over in the other bed was doing much the same. I was thinking. Looking back on it now, I suppose I must admit that it was nothing anyone should dignify with the name of thinking. I was just letting one crazy thought chase another through my head.

I kept going back in my mind over the afternoon and evening. I was trying to remember. I was working on everything I could remember. Who had been where when? Who had been with whom? Had there been moments of tension?

I was thinking about the campus prowl I had done with Larry. It had to have been during the time we'd been doing that. It had been then that she had been sucked into going up to the room and then that she had been fed the doctored drink.

Why had it been our room? Because it had been empty? There had been other empty rooms. I was remembering the people who had still been down in the Quad when we'd gone up to the room. Their rooms would also have been empty. Could it have been that those others had read the instruction sheet and that ours had been the only room both empty and unlocked?

I came to thinking about the hour or more that Larry and I had been separated. There had been time then for going back to the Quad and up to the room with Sooey. It was crazy. In the first place I knew Larry too well. Also it was Larry who was saying murder. It was Larry who was piecing together all the evidence for it. A man doesn't assemble murder evidence and present it against himself. It was insanity for that thought even to come stalking through my mind. Of course, he was a doctor. Of course, he knew how it could be done. That didn't mean anything. It couldn't mean anything.

He was in that other bed. Was he thinking about me this same way I was thinking about him? He had been so careful about not telling anything I might not want told. What would that have been for? He would be thinking that I wouldn't have put the bottle back in my bag. He would be thinking that I wouldn't have told where I'd found it. He would be thinking he knew me too well. He would be thinking it's crazy.

He would also be thinking about the kid. Why should the boy have been so scared? Could it be that he had recognized one of us?

CHAPTER 3

All those, of course, were night thoughts. Anyone can have them and then, in the morning, looking at them in the light of day, he laughs at himself. Over such nonsense I lost sleep? I kept telling myself that I was an idiot, but I couldn't get away from the feeling that it wasn't quite as it had been between Larry and me. It was nothing you could put a finger on, but it was there, just that little constraint, a touch of unease that lay between us.

I was telling myself that it had to be my discomfort over having even for a moment had those thoughts about him. He would be feeling a like discomfort over having had those same thoughts about me. That had to be what I was sensing. It couldn't be anything more than that. Even while I was telling myself all this stuff, however, I would catch myself trying to recollect. I was working at reconstructing what it had been between Sooey and all of us, between Sooey and all too many of us. Could it have been different with Larry? Had his been something apart from the universal experience?

There were some lines from a Stephen Vincent Benét poem that kept turning up in my head. Bob used to quote them back in those days. Bob used to be the funnel through which poetry came to Larry and me.

"Sweet as secret thievery I kiss her all I can
"While somebody above remarks, 'That's not a nice young
    man.' "

So we had none of us been "nice young men." Surely, however, there had been nothing that could come to murder, much less murder after twenty years.

Mrs. Mulligan gave us breakfast and, what with the dean being most undeanlike and the merriment of their brood of kids, there was nothing solemn or dark hovering over the breakfast table. After breakfast Larry and I walked back to the Quad. For most of the walk we were saying nothing. We were almost there when Larry broke the silence.

"Do you feel much like going back? Do you want to take up again where we left off on this old-buddy crap?" he asked.

"What else is there for us to do?"

"I don't know. We'll have to stick around. I can't see how we can do anything else."

"Particularly if you're right about its being murder," I said.

"It's murder, Matt. I've been trying to argue myself away from it, but nothing else makes any kind of sense."

"You think murder makes sense?"

"It fits the evidence. The symptoms are there. You have to read the symptoms. She was building something and it fell in on her. If she wasn't going to drink them, she didn't have to take every drink that was pushed at her. All the time yesterday, when we were going around with Slammer and Bob, you saw the way Slammer handled it. She passed more often than not, and she wasn't the only one. Most of the girls were doing the same, pacing themselves and making no pretense that they were doing anything else."

"Different women, different ways," I said without any faith in what I was saying.

"And Sooey's way got her killed," Larry said.

In the Quad we walked into a reception I could have done without. We were the killers. Everyone was being very funny about it, but a bad joke endlessly repeated gets no funnier as each wit takes his individual whack at it.

Slammer and Bob were there and they, at least, weren't laughing. If for nothing else, I loved them for that; and nothing had to be said for me to know that Larry was with me there. We were a long time before we could break loose from the gruesome hilarity. We were still stuck with it when Ham Roberts came into the Quad carrying a small parcel. He had been off somewhere in town. Glad was nowhere in evidence. He was also not laughing. I caught myself almost liking him for it.

The feeling didn't last. By his reaction to Sooey's death he cured me of it immediately. The bastard had the nerve to give it the wages-of-sin touch. I was aching to poke him one, but Bob had the better way of handling it. Bob's was the verbal poke.

"How comes it that you're still alive?" he asked.

I expected that Ham would take that with some sort of big-man-between-the-sheets swagger, but he didn't. He resented it. Slammer hurried forward to do the wifely thing: she changed the subject.

"Where's Glad?" she asked. "She wasn't at breakfast. I haven't seen her this morning."

"She'll be down soon," Ham said, "as soon as I've gotten this stuff up to her. She's had a little accident."

He was waving his little package about. This was the good husband who had been running an errand for the little woman.

"She hasn't hurt herself?"

If it had been anyone else, I would have been looking for a touch of derision in this show of sympathy and concern, but it was Slammer. The sympathy and concern were genuine.

Ham went into a long explanation. Glad had never before spent a night in a place like this. For Glad the dorm was slumming. She had never in her whole life slept in a room that didn't have its connecting bath. She had never even known that there were people who lived this way.

"And the room itself," he said. "She's never had to put up with such close quarters. She can't get used to having no room to turn around in. She keeps bumping into things and coming away black and blue. She walked straight into an open closet door and gave herself a black eye. I've been down the street to get her some stuff she can paint over it so it won't show so much. She has to have it. She just won't come out of the room with a shiner."

"Poor thing," Slammer said. "You go right up to her. You're keeping her waiting."

"She's lying down with ice on it," Ham said.

"What a shame," Slammer said. "Is there anything I can do for her?"

"Oh, no. Thanks very much. She'll be fine. She's always . . ."

He got that far with it and then thought better of what he'd been about to say.

"If there is anything I can do, let me know."

Slammer was jumping in on it and covering his confusion. I suppose, however, that he could read in our faces the tenor of what we were supplying to fill the gap of what he was leaving unsaid. He evidently felt some compulsion to feed us a version of his own making.

"She's always quick to bounce back," he said. "She'll be fine."

He took off into the dorm with his little package. I suppose Larry and I should have been grateful to him. He had provided a diversion. His story was being passed around the Quad, and nobody was showing any faith in it. I don't know that he could have done better if he had thought up some new gag, but the Open Door Policy has been around too long. You'd have to be Ham Roberts to try to get by on that one. While the rest of the gang was having its new laugh, Bob moved to pull us out of the Quad into something more private.

"It's dog-hair time," he said. "Up in our room the matutinal Bloody Marys. I'm countering Ham's bruised Glad with my Bloody Mary."

"I'm taking some words out of her mouth, my fancy-talking mate. Call me Slammer."

"Bloody Slammers?" Bob tried it for size and shuddered.

They had Bloody Marys going on the hard-stuff bar down in the Quad, but it was more than worth the flight of stairs to get off by ourselves.

"The word about Sooey got around mighty quick," I said.

"All the activity next door in your room," Slammer said.

"People noticed, plus missing the two of you at breakfast," Bob added. "They asked questions. They got answers. The word got around. It was all over the dining room at breakfast."

"What activity?" I asked.

"Bed taken out. Another bed brought in. Beds being carried out and in through the Quad," Slammer said. "People questioned the kids who were doing the hauling."

"What was it, Larry?" Bob asked. "Coronary? Stroke?"

Larry was about to answer, but when I kicked him in the ankle, he swallowed it.

We had left the door to the room standing open. Don't ask me why, unless it might have been that, without thinking, we had reverted to ancient habit. In our time it had been a serious offense if you had a woman in your room after six in the evening. Before six o'clock, during what must have been presumed the hours of impotence, it was permitted, but the door had to be left ajar and she had to have at least one foot on the floor.

I had spotted someone out in the corridor. One of the undergraduates was out there. He was evidently one of those still in residence among the rooms that had been commandeered for us. He was obviously not that offensive linebacker who had been surprised under the shower in the Ladies'. He was a good hundred pounds short of making the weight, and he didn't look at all the type who might have had so lighthearted a disregard for the niceties of gender.

I have never seen a more proper-looking young man. Except for his fresh-faced youth, he looked all wrong for an undergraduate. In that world of T-shirt and jeans, he was wearing a complete suit, a button-down blue oxford shirt, and old-school tie neatly tied. His shoes were shined and his hair was neatly shorn to that crew-cut length that even among us old boys had long since been abandoned for the blown-dry and the sideburns.

He looked like nothing out of his generation and not even like anything out of ours. You'd have to hark back to the jazz-age twenties to find his like. He had the manners to go with his looks. As we turned toward him, he wished us a polite good morning. He came and stood in the doorway to ask if we were having a good reunion.

Bob invited him in. He offered him a Bloody Mary. With politeness so exquisite that it could even have been a travesty of etiquette, the kid declined both. Bob was matching him courtesy for courtesy, introducing him to Slammer and then performing introductions all around. The kid said his name was Rick Dowling and he had to be on his way. He would be seeing us around. He told us to enjoy ourselves.

As soon as young Dowling had pulled out, Bob repeated his question. This time Larry waited with his answer until I had shut the door.

"No need to keep this open," I said, "and Slammer doesn't even have to keep her feet on the floor."

"It wasn't natural," Larry said. "She was murdered."

"Sooey?" Bob couldn't believe it. "You must be joking. Who would murder Sooey and whatever for?"

Larry outlined for them what he was calling the symptoms. They listened in startled silence. At one point, however, Slammer broke in on him. It was when he was telling them about the games Sooey had been playing with her drinks.

"I noticed that," she said, "and I didn't need whiskey in my shoes to call it to my attention. Once I'd noticed, I kept watching her, and it was fascinating. I thought it would be part of her good-time-girl image that she drank with all the boys. I thought perhaps she wanted only the image and none of the substance. I never dreamt that there could be anything sinister about it."

"I didn't either," Larry said, "not until afterward. After she was dead and I began piecing together all the little oddities, this was just another thing. It fitted in."

"She used to drink them down in the old days, and she could hold them, too," Bob said.

"Twenty years—a person's capacity can change," Slammer said.

Larry shook his head. "More likely in the other direction," he said, "even all the way to liver damage and delirium tremens. The capacity increases. Not too infrequently it ups to damaging levels."

"Why didn't you come over and wake us?" Bob asked.

"What for?"

"I don't know," Bob said. "We stand together—all that sort of thing." Bob had always been awesomely articulate, but in a moment of sentiment he went tongue-tied. "Suppose you guys had been suspected," he said.

"We still can be," Larry said. "As soon as anyone else starts seeing it for murder, we can be."

"You should have come to us before you called anyone," Slammer said. "Bob's right. We could have said you were with us all the time."

"Unnecessary," Larry said, "and dishonest."

"Also," I said, "useless. We didn't go hide ourselves away. We did the reunion prowl. People saw us all over the campus and they saw that you weren't with us."

"Then you have alibis," Bob said.

"We probably could piece some together," I told him. "That is if our large assortment of drunken friends remember that much of what went on last night."

"It's nonsense anyhow," Larry said. "We don't need alibis. There's no murder evidence that doesn't come from Matt and me. Would we work all that hard to accuse ourselves?"

"You wouldn't have been taking all that guff from our buddies downstairs," Bob said.

"We've taken it," I said. "We've survived."

"And all that's been wiped out by Glad's shiner," Larry added.

"Yes," Bob said. "How about that? There's a guy who hasn't changed."

We were interrupted by a knock at the door. It was young Rick Dowling back. Now he had a camera with him and it was a spectacular one. If we didn't mind, he wanted a picture of us.

"Why?" Slammer asked.

"Because you're photogenic, ma'am," the kid said.

"Of course," Slammer said, "but they're not."

"You can't have everything," young Rick said.

He went on to explain that he had stayed on through reunion time even though he had finished all his exams. He was working. A lot of the kids stay on for that. Reunions are run on undergraduate help. They do the bartending. They pull the levers on the beer pumps. They wait tables, and they perform other such services for the comfort and convenience of the returning alumni. Their working uniform consists of chewed-off shorts and T-shirts. For a working stiff, Dowling was much overdressed.

He explained that. He wasn't in the employ of one of the returning classes. He was self-employed.

"Reunion pictures," he said. "Magazines and newspapers buy them and I can sell a lot of prints right here. Pictures of yourselves, pictures of your friends—you take them home as souvenirs."

"What do we look like?" Larry asked. "*Playboy* or *Business Week*?"

"Beautiful people," the kid said.

He took several shots, and he was impressively expert in the way he went about it. He had all sorts of equipment and he worked with professional assurance and zip. When he had finished, he thanked us elaborately and took off.

The rest of the day passed uneventfully. People fell into the standard routines. The golfers golfed. The even more energetic hit the tennis courts. The four of us hung together, and it worked fine since we were just right for doubles. The bridge players dealt cards and bickered. There was a poker game in one of the dorm rooms and a crap game in another. The serious drinkers allowed nothing to interfere with their seriousness.

It was during the cocktail hour that our buddy, the dean, turned up. He cued Larry and me in on the autopsy findings. Larry, of course, had called it—alcohol and barbiturates.

"When everyone is here," Mulligan said, "I'll make an announcement. I'll wait till you go in to dinner."

"Announcement of what?" I asked.

"The findings. People should know. We don't want it happening again. It can, you know, all too easily."

Larry looked at me and I looked at him. His look was questioning. I spoke.

"Except," I said, "that we're pretty sure it was murder."

Dean Mulligan jumped.

"Hey," he said. "You don't want to go around talking that way."

"We don't go around talking any way," Larry said, "but we're saying it to you. The postmortem findings show that she had been in good health, don't they?"

"They do, but I don't see."

"Fill the man in, Doc," I said.

Larry took the dean through it step by step, feeding him the whole package. Mulligan took it in appalled silence.

"It just doesn't seem possible," he said after Larry had finished.

"Why doesn't it?" I asked. "Because the grand old place doesn't educate murderers?"

"The widow of a classmate? What could anyone have against the widow of a classmate?"

"She happens to have been a lot more than that," I said.

I wasn't comfortable about telling him what more and how widely distributed. Larry took care of that. He explained and he brought to the explanation the most beautiful clinical detachment.

Our friend the dean showed an almost offensive degree of astonishment. It seemed to stagger him that in our time we could have been capable of it. He made a quick recovery and got busy playing it down.

"Dorm bull-sessions," he said. "I haven't forgotten what they were like. Always a lot of boasting and a high degree of bullshit that has to be discounted."

"It's firsthand knowledge for too many of us," I said. "Too many of us were there. She was like community property. You may be thinking that what we're handing you is more bull-session crap, but the lady's dead and we have only kind memories of her. There's no kiss-and-tell fun in it, not at this stage."

"With a reputation like that she could hardly have had a hold on anyone," the dean said, "and surely not after twenty years?"

He decided that in the few words he would speak to the class he was going to pretend that Larry and I hadn't said anything. So he talked of an accident and warned against the danger of another such accident. On his way out he stopped for another word with Larry and me. He asked us to say nothing of our suspicions.

"I'll take it up with President Dale and we'll have to tell the police," he said. "They'll undoubtedly want to talk to you, and whatever announcement they choose to make will be up to them. Meanwhile let's leave it as I have it. I think that will be best."

I did have the passing thought that maybe people should be warned against taking a drink from anyone, but it seemed silly. Although I kept asking myself the question that the dean had asked, I could come up with no reasonable answer for why anyone could have wanted Sooey out of the way. I was telling myself, nevertheless, that there had to be a reason. I couldn't believe that there was a killer among us who, with unmotivated malice, would go around fixing people lethal drinks.

Of course Dean Danny's announcement switched all the table talk away from the remember-when sort of thing that is the reunion standard. It seemed that everyone knew someone who had made just this same mistake and everyone had to tell everyone else about it. Nobody seemed at all aware that his or her story came all too close to being a duplicate of all the others.

Only Ham Roberts gave it a different touch. We were at long tables for ten, and Ham and Glad were at the next table. He had his back to us with Florence Hoyt beside him. Culver Hoyt and Glad Roberts were opposite them and facing us. I had a perfect view of the Glad Roberts mouse. It was a beauty. The stuff Ham had brought her from the drugstore may have masked the color, but neither ice nor makeup had reduced the swelling.

There was also a perceptible coolness between Glad and Ham. I tried thinking that I could be imagining the chill and that it was something I was manufacturing out of my conviction that it was not a door but her husband that had been the mouse hanger. I was telling myself that he had changed not at all.

As though to convince me that I was right in my assumption, Ham made his comment on the death. He just about shouted it. Evidently he thought it was so great that he wanted nobody to miss it. It was the story about the two tigers at a bar drinking martinis. Down at the other end of the bar there was a beautiful blonde. One of the tigers couldn't take his eyes off her.

"See that blonde?" he said to his fellow tiger.

"I see her. Some stuff."

"I'd like to go right over there and eat her up."

"Why don't you. I'll have another martini while I'm waiting."

The hungry tiger trotted down the bar, perched on a barstool beside the blonde, and started a conversation. After some brief preliminaries he ate her up. Licking his chops, he returned to the other tiger and ordered another martini. While he was drinking it, he began to feel sleepy.

"I guess I'm not the tiger I used to be," he said. "I don't seem to be able to hold my drinks any more. I'm about to fall asleep."

"Nonsense," his friend said. "It isn't the martinis. It's the bar bitch you ate."

"Get it?" Ham shouted. "Bar bitch you ate—barbiturate."

He laughed and laughed, knocking himself out. Some of the wives laughed with him. They would be the ones who didn't know the score. Otherwise it was all frozen silence. Culver Hoyt broke it. He jumped to his feet, leaned across the table, and slapped Ham's face. It was the flat of his hand against Ham's left cheek followed by the quick backhander to the right cheek.

Glad, who had not laughed at the joke, was laughing now. Happily for her, Ham was in no shape to notice. He might well have closed her other eye for her. Instead he lunged at Culver. Glasses toppled and broke. Dishes shattered. The table tipped over and all the people sitting on that side of it went down in a welter of spilled liquor, spilled food, broken glass, shattered crockery, and cascading cutlery.

The lunge that upset the table carried Ham across it, bringing him down on Culver with his hands reaching for Culver's throat. Culver, however, was ready for him. He had a knee up, and, as Ham came in, he rammed it hard into Ham's groin. Up to that time, if you had asked me where you should go to see dirty fighting that neatly executed, I would have recommended the back alleys of a tough town like Glasgow. What I was seeing then was telling me that you can do as well if you hang around under the arches of one of our more prestigious institutions of learning.

I would have liked to have stood back and watched the fracas. I was perfectly placed for watching, right at ringside; but it wasn't to be. After all, there was Glad Roberts to be pulled out from under all that, and there were other women who had also been sitting on the wrong side of the battleground. They also needed extricating.

We rallied round. We pulled them away. Slammer and some of the other wives moved in to lend a hand, scraping the peas and the gravy off the bosoms of the innocent victims. A lot of the guys rushed in to wrestle the combatants apart, but it was an undergraduate waiter who acted effectively. He hauled Ham off Culver, and with one big, meaty hand he held him off while with the other he pulled Culver to his feet and thwarted all the efforts he was making to return to the charge.

The kid was a great specimen of the way they are growing them these days. He stood a good six feet five, and if he weighed anything under 260, it could only be an ounce or two nobody's going to quibble about. He had to be the offensive linebacker the ladies had encountered in the shower. If the old place could have boasted more than one of him, they would have been better placed in the football standings.

He held Ham and Culver apart. If they'd had a stone wall between them, they couldn't have been more effectively separated. He had them reduced to words and in that department neither of them was at all inventive. Son of a bitch, repeated often enough, loses any force it might once have had.

Meanwhile the young giant was trying to reason with them.

"Gentlemen," he kept saying. "Remember that you're gentlemen. Remember that there are ladies present. Remember that it's only because I was well brought up and I've been taught to respect my elders that I'm not handing the two of you a couple of knuckle sandwiches. Remember that if you go on this way, you may have me unlearning all that respect I've been taught."

All of this was being said in a silken purr and with the gentlest of indulgent smiles. So what's wrong with the young? I'm ready to fight anyone who says that lad can't shower anywhere he likes.

All the while there was Glad Roberts. Her dress and her jewelry were besmeared but she wasn't taking any notice. She laughed and laughed. She shook with it. She sobbed with it. She was all the way out of control, but it wasn't hysteria, it was unadulterated mirth. She had never enjoyed anything that much, maybe not even the biggest of her emeralds.

The kid and his two belligerents were at an impasse. He could hold them apart, but he was getting nowhere with persuading them to simmer down. The three of us—Larry and Bob and I—moved in to help him. It could have been yesterday the way the old teamwork came back to us. It was automatic. We just clicked into it. No signals. We didn't need any.

We just closed in and pulled Culver away. We left Ham to the jolly young giant. Removed from the scene of combat, Culver began cooling down. By gradual stages he became aware of his own encrustation of peas and gravy. From that he moved to a growing concern for his wife.

"Where's Florence?" he said. "Is she all right?"

We took him upstairs and delivered him to their room. She was already up there. Culver went in and we waited out in the hall. Slammer, who had been in the room with Florence, came out and headed straight for Bob.

"We're moving," she said.

Bob grinned at her.

"It was a great fight," he said. "Homer should be living in this hour. Don't pretend you didn't enjoy it."

"I didn't enjoy it," Slammer said. "It was ugly and it's horrible for poor Florence. We can't leave them here in this room."

"What's wrong with the room?"

"Nothing. It's a twin to ours, but guess who they have next door."

"Mr. and Mrs. Hamilton Roberts?"

"You're real quick, husband mine. So we're swapping rooms with them."

"Why we?" Bob asked. "I like our neighborhood. We're with the best people. Why should we go slumming?"

"Because I've told her that we'll swap," Slammer said. "She's packing them up right now."

"Without consulting me? What's happened to our perfect marriage?"

"Stop clowning and come and help me pack."

She had taken command and she was holding it. Turning to Larry and me, she gave us our orders. We were to stay where we were. Somebody had to stand guard until the transfer had been made. After all, Ham could be coming up to his room at any time. We weren't to forget that Glad would be in need of repairs.

"I can't expect you to be as good at it as that remarkable child in the dining room," she said, "but there are two of you. You should be able to prevent bloodshed. Just stay here until we're moved. You won't be missing anything but dessert and, as soon as we're moved in, we'll give you a drink. That will compensate you for missing the jello."

Bob was still grumbling about the change in neighbors. She made short work of that.

"So you're henpecked," she said. "So what? You know very well that when we aren't in their room, they'll be here in ours. Also, even though I love them dearly, there are other people. We shouldn't be too seclusive."

"And what if he gives me wife-beating lessons?" Bob asked.

"I'll just go to her for how-to-hit-the-old-man-for-emeralds lessons, not to speak of laughing lessons."

With that she hauled him off to pack. Larry and I mounted guard, but neither Glad nor Ham showed. After all, he had no need for repairs. None of the dinner had spilled on him, and in her hilarity Glad was evidently past caring. There was no reason for them not to stay for dessert and coffee. Jewelry is easily washed. It was also more than likely that our young peacemaker would be keeping them where they were, affording all parties ample time for head cooling.

Nobody of our crowd showed. The only one who came by was that assiduous photographer, Rick Dowling. He turned up complete with all his picture-taking equipment. The kid was bubbling over with excitement. He'd gotten beautiful shots of the fight. He was now bent on taking some close-ups of Culver Hoyt in all his food-smeared disarray. We dissuaded him.

"I wouldn't," Larry said.

"Unless you're hungry for a thick lip," I said. "This is no time to go tangling with Killer Culver."

Rick looked thoughtful.

"He does do a first-class ear-ringer, doesn't he?" he said.

"And we," Larry told him, "are of the generation that believes in a heavy hand for the young. We spank the impertinence out of them."

The kid sighed.

"They'd make a great picture," he said. "He and the lady with all the rocks."

"And you're likely to end up with a busted camera."

That was my contribution. Larry took a more direct approach.

"Do you move along," he asked, "or do we move you?"

He took a step toward the boy. The old teamwork routine took over. I moved with him.

"I'm going," Rick Dowling said.

He went.

"Were you ready to rough him up?" I asked Larry.

"Weren't you?"

"Young Mr. Dowling is not my favorite boy."

"I never thought we'd see the day," Larry said, "when the old place would take to raising paparazzi."

"Watch it," I said. "You're beginning to sound like an old curmudgeon. We were all kinds and they're all kinds now."

"I prefer the kind that broke them up downstairs," Larry said.

It was about then that Florence and Culver opened their door. He'd done a quick change, and he began hauling their bags out to the hall. We gave him a hand with them. So it was the four of us together for the move over to our entry. Although considerably cooled down, Culver was still growling.

He was doing the defender-of-pure-womanhood act. It was no kind of thing to say before ladies. Also the poor woman was dead and no decent man says things like that about a woman, living or dead. She had been married to a classmate and that made her one of us. Somebody had to rise to her defense. So Culver Hoyt was Galahad and there wasn't a one of the rest of us fit for a seat at the Round Table. He wished everybody hadn't been so quick to pull him away from Ham Roberts. The louse should have had a lot more than he got.

"He has no respect for women," Culver said. "He has no respect for anything. I'm ashamed to think he's a member of our class. He's every kind of louse. He's a wife beater, too. You saw that eye his wife has. She didn't run into any door. I can guarantee that."

Florence chimed in. It seems that she was his witness. Right there in the next room she had heard things during the night. She had heard the poor woman scream and cry.

"He was beating her," she said. "I just knew he was. A

woman might run into a door, but she doesn't go on and on running into a door. He was beating her." She turned to her husband. "Didn't I tell you when you came up last night? I was sorry you weren't there. I was sorry there was nobody to go in and stop the brute."

So Culver wished he'd been there. He would certainly have gone next door and given the louse what for.

By the time we had them moved, we'd had all we could have wanted of that song and dance. So Larry and I were everybody's moving men. We helped Bob carry his and Slammer's bags to their new quarters. That brought us face to face with Glad and Ham.

"He's scared, huh?" Ham said. "Well, that's smart. If he has any sense, he's going to stay far away from me."

"Ham, my lad," Bob said, "that tiger story of yours is very old. If you will tell old jokes, you must be ready to take the consequences."

"Old or new," Ham said. "It was appropriate. You can't say it wasn't appropriate."

"Neil Neecey," Bob said, "thought it was grossly inappropriate."

"Neil who?" Ham asked, "and whoever he is, what's he got to do with it?"

"He's a defender of womanhood," Slammer said, "and he speaks only good of the dead."

With a wave of his hand Ham dismissed the noble character.

"Don't know him," he said. "Never heard of him. He wasn't even in our class."

We left it at that. None of us had any great interest in enlightening Ham Roberts. These names Bob whipped up for people had never been for general circulation. Sooey Generous had been an in-joke shared only with Larry and me. Now with Culver Hoyt thundering around in his disapproval of speaking ill of the dead, even though Culver wasn't doing it in the original Latin, it was inevitable that Bob should name him Neil Neecey. In our little group he might have been destined to be Neil forevermore.

It worked out just as Slammer had predicted. Virtually any time we had the impulse to withdraw from the mob scene in the Quad, it would be the four of us in their room or in ours. The ties that had once been close hadn't been loosened by the years.

Despite all his bluster, Ham Roberts was the one who showed great care in avoiding another confrontation with Dr. Culver Hoyt. Culver, on the other hand, seemed disposed toward keeping the thing alive. He was being Neil Neecey all over the place. Wherever he could grab an ear he filled it with an account of the gallantry of his attitude to what he persisted in calling the gentler sex and of his reverential attitude toward the dead.

CHAPTER 4

As the evening wore on, things dropped back into reunion routine. The general topic of conversation throughout the dorm and down in the Quad, however, was, of course, the sudden death of Sooey Generous. I was beginning to wonder what people would have found to talk about if it hadn't happened. Among the four of us we were a little uncomfortable with the way old-time habit kept us calling her Sooey, but we comforted ourselves with the thought that to change that would to a great extent be divorcing ourselves from our memories of her. We discussed it and agreed that she was worth remembering, and that as she had been alive.

Our friend the dean dropped around again to cut Larry and me out of the herd. He had to talk to us. Since it was to be confidential talk, it couldn't be done down in the Quad. I've already told you about the reunion decibel level. If a man was to be heard, he had to shout. Shouted confidences are not likely to remain confidential.

We took him up to our room and gave him a drink. That didn't take us away from the noise; the whole building thundered with it, but up there with the door shut we could shout at each other and not be heard beyond the confines of the room.

He had talked to the president and they had talked to the town authorities—the mayor and the chief of police.

Although the university president, a man of science, was impressed with and perturbed by Larry's evidence and our conclusions, neither the mayor nor the police chief could see any reason for them to take any action.

"I don't know about the mayor," the dean said, "but the chief, who after all has professional expertise in these matters, sees nothing in it."

"In our day," I said, "the local cops went around loaded to the eyeballs with expertise on the antics of the drunk and disorderly. In all of the four years we were here I don't remember any murders coming their way. Have things changed that much?"

"Murders," the dean said. "No. The big difference is we get rapes these days, but the best opinion has it that the actual incidence may not have increased. It could be that it's only that women are less shy about reporting it than they used to be."

"Rape," Larry said, "is beside the point. I'm betting that your police chief is the complete amateur when it comes to murder."

The dean shrugged.

"We've done our part," he said. "The chief's the man in charge. I don't see that there's anything more that we can do or should do."

"And we don't want to give reunions a bad name," Larry said.

The dean didn't like that. You couldn't expect that he would. He froze up on us.

"We can't tell you to remain silent," he said. "We'd prefer that you did, but we can't tell you to. I suppose you must do or say whatever you think necessary."

"And to no effect except to spoil the party," Larry said. "Okay. Forget that we ever opened our mouths."

"Don't feel like that," the dean said. "We do appreciate your telling us."

It wasn't long before his appreciation took on greater depth. We were on the stairs with him headed back down to the Quad, when we heard the screams. They were coming from the next entry. You won't understand this unless I give you a quick once-over on the dormitory floor plan. Although it's one building strung around the four sides of the quadrangle, it's broken up into a series of separate entries, each with its individual stairwell and each accessible only from the open green of the quadrangle. From entry to entry there is no interior communication except down in the basement of the dorm. Down there a continuous series of linked corridors runs the full circuit.

That we heard the screams at all from where we were— on the stairs in the adjacent entry—was possible only because they happened to come during one of those brief intervals when the rock band was taking a breather between sets. It was a woman screaming. Her screams were not only loud. They carried a full cargo of fright.

The three of us pelted down the stairs and out into the Quad. For that stretch Larry and I passed the dean and left him to come slogging along behind us. I don't know that we were that much faster on our feet. I'm inclined to think that the difference lay in the fact that Larry and I were true believers, highly motivated. The dean, I think, was just wishing that he could have been some place else.

Once we were out the entry door, however, nobody was gaining on anyone else. The doorway to that next entry was packed solid with classmates, the massed chivalry of us old-timers rushing to the aid of a damsel in distress. Taking the lead, I cut a way for us through the massed bodies. It took a little elbowing, but I had a magic formula and I was getting far better results from that than I could ever have achieved with the elbow.

"Gangway," I kept yelling. "Gangway. We have the dean here. Make way for the dean."

The screaming had stopped and I didn't like thinking about the way it had stopped. There had been no fade-out. It had been a sharp cut-off. I couldn't imagine anything but that the lady had been silenced in mid-scream.

Dean was the magic word. Guys made way for us. The three of us ran up the stairs. In each entry on each floor there are six rooms. One room on the second floor had its door standing ajar and its doorway stuffed with our aging fellow-gallants. They opened a path for the dean and the three of us made it into the room.

There Dr. Culver Hoyt was in charge. The woman was stretched out on one of the two beds and Culver was ministering to her. Larry dove in to work with him. I had to push aside the thought that at least she would have a second opinion before Neil Neecey could get her scheduled for one of his hysterectomies.

I had seen her around, although I didn't know her. I was assuming she was a wife I hadn't yet met and wondered where her husband might be. There were plenty of the buddies in the room and plenty crowding the corridor outside, but they seemed to be just guys. I could spot nobody who seemed to be taking that special proprietary interest that could be expected of a husband.

She was out cold, but even to my layman's eye it was evident that this would be the whole of it. She wasn't dead. With two eminent MDs ministering to her, she came around in short order. That is she came back to consciousness. It took considerable further ministering before she was back to anything like coherence.

"A burglar," she said. "I came up to powder my nose and I surprised a burglar in here. He attacked me."

She hadn't seen him. She hadn't seen anyone. She had opened the door and the shock of what she saw then had started her screaming. Until she spoke of what she saw I don't know that any of us had been taking any notice of it. I do know that, speaking for myself, I had missed out on it entirely. I was ready to say we all had. We'd been focused on the unconscious woman, and none of us could have had any knowledge of whether the lady's habits were neat or sloppy.

Once she had called our attention to the room's wild state of disarray, however, I immediately recognized that it could never have been of her own doing. There is no woman anywhere—and for that matter few men—who could be that much a slob. Suitcases lay empty and yawning. Everything they had contained lay strewn around the room. Most of it lay crumpled on the floor: stockings, slips, shoes, blouses, nightgowns, skirts, dresses, toilet articles.

More than that, there appeared to have been some vandalism as well. There had been a box of what I took to be some sort of talcum powder. It had been dumped. The powder emptied out of it was all over the place. Never but once had I seen anything like it and that had been when a pet monkey kept by a woman I knew had run amok through her things. When, however, she had surprised the beast at it, the monkey hadn't handed her the neatly placed blow to the head that would knock her unconscious.

This woman had taken just such a blow. Larry located the bruise. She had opened the door and, shocked by the sight of all that disarray, she had screamed. Her assailant, who had evidently been concealed behind the door, knocked her cold and made his escape. She hadn't seen him.

There was no way of knowing, of course, just what might have been taken. That was going to have to wait until the victim had regained her composure and would be in shape to put her stuff in some kind of order for taking inventory.

The dean introduced himself to her and one of the guys introduced her to the dean. She was Alberta Smith. The guy explained that she was the widow of one of our late classmates, Jim Smith.

It was Larry's opinion, and Culver concurred in it, that she had suffered no lasting damage. They were speaking only, of course, of physical damage. They recommended that she attempt no exertion. She was just to rest quietly until she had recovered from the shock.

"Not here," she said.

"No," Larry agreed. "Certainly not here."

"I'd like to go home," she said, "just pack up and go home."

"Not till you're rested," Larry said. "At least overnight, and we'll see how you are in the morning."

"Not here," she repeated.

The dean took a hand. Mrs. Smith would go to the university infirmary.

"You will be comfortable there, Mrs. Smith," he said.

She knew the infirmary and she took to that suggestion happily. The infirmary has always been a luxury institution. Over the years it has been the favorite project of the wives and mothers of alumni and the mothers and aunts of undergraduates. They keep it lavishly funded. There's no place where patients are given more pampering. I gathered that Alberta Smith was about to get some of her own back.

A couple of the women had worked their way into the room and they took over on putting together the few things Alberta might want to take to the infirmary with her. They also began neating the place up a bit. At that point the dean had a thought. He took it up with me. Larry and I, after all, were the ones he knew best in our gang, and Larry was being medical. I was on the loose.

"Not all of this stuff would be hers," he said. "Who is her roommate in here? The woman ought to be told. She'll want to sort out her own things."

I didn't know, but it did seem reasonable that the housing committee might have paired up widows just as they had paired up bachelors. I turned to the guy who had identified her for us and passed the question on to him.

"She has the room alone," he said. "Mrs. Graystock had been in here with her."

That was a piece of intelligence I felt the dean should have, but by the time I'd picked it up, he was off across the room and well into his song and dance about the increasingly mobile underworld characters who come into town to prey on the happily careless reunion drunks. His remarks were provoking a lot of middle-aged head-shaking. You know that garbage about how the world used to be a better place when you and I were young.

Only Culver Hoyt spoke up to take issue with this comfortable theorizing. He was now letting Larry take on all of the ministering-to-the-stricken stuff. After all, Culver was a surgeon and the conditions were hardly suited to his specialties, whether delivering an infant or snapping out a uterus.

"It was no outsider," he said. "Nobody can get in here but people back to one of the reunions, just them and the undergraduates who live here in the dorm."

It was a good argument. I thought he had the dean there. Mulligan, however, was a better man than I'd been recognizing. He had a ready answer. It was true that each of the reunion areas was kept blocked off with only one entrance and that manned by university proctors or other beefy security personnel. Nobody was admitted except people wearing reunion uniforms. The only exception was made for undergrads who were working that reunion or the few kids who showed ID that established them as living in the dorm. They, of course, couldn't be barred from their own rooms.

Culver was taking his own middle-aged view of the thing. The old place wasn't what it had been. The admissions office was taking in all kinds of riff-raff. In our time it had been a place for gentlemen. Now it was a nest of guttersnipes. They had no respect for anyone or anything. I had a hunch that there might be one undergraduate he had specifically in mind, the big boy who had imposed the peace when Culver had been doing his Neil Neecey act with his hands on Ham's throat.

Mulligan, however, moved quickly too. He called attention to the fact that the younger alumni, classes only a year or two out, didn't go in for elaborate reunion costumes. They held down the expenses. Uniform for them would consist of chewed-off shorts and a T-shirt of some distinctive color.

"Crooks come into town," he said. "They look around and they spot a uniform like that. It's all too easy to fake. So they're walking in and out of every reunion on campus. They only have to avoid the class whose uniform they've imitated. We do our best to control it, but we can't do the impossible."

He launched into his refrain about keeping doors locked

and leaving nothing of value lying around. I wondered whether he could have forgotten his own undergraduate years. There hadn't been a locked door in any of the dorms that we couldn't open by slipping a knife in to push the lock tongue back. The doors and the locks were still exactly as they had been. There had been no change.

I worked my way across the room to his side. It took some doing. The room in truth was less full of people than it had been; Larry had demanded air for the patient. It nonetheless took a lot of careful stepping and sidestepping to avoid putting a shoe down on one piece of frippery or another and to dodge the greater concentrations of the spilled powder.

As soon as I'd reached his ear, I gave it to him.

"You'll want to take it into your thinking," I said, "that she was in here alone. She lost her roommate. She had been rooming with Mrs. Graystock."

Culver Hoyt, who had Mulligan's other ear for his undergraduate-culprit line, was quicker than the dean to pick up on what I was saying.

"Bad luck room," he said.

I had other ideas about it and they were less simple-minded. Dean Mulligan, who had been dealing with the thoughts Larry and I had been shoving at him, was in a position to read my mind. He read it.

"There's nothing of Mrs. Graystock's in here now," he said. "I had all her things brought to me and they're locked up in my office. Her roommate packed it for us. That would have been Mrs. Smith."

He might have been thinking that he'd given me all I needed to rid myself of the idea that was bugging me or it could have been that he just wanted to shut me up, but with an air of satisfaction at having put the lid on that, he moved across to the bed. He had some questions for Alberta Smith. He couldn't ask her to sort through her stuff and tell him what if anything was missing; Larry would have had his ears if he had so much as tried. Larry scowled at the few questions Mulligan did ask, but he let him go that far.

Were there any valuables that she had left in the room?

Alberta Smith was an old hand at reunions. Over the years she had attended many of them with her Jim. She knew better than to bring anything of value. It was not that kind of party.

"It's all so informal," she said. "It would be vulgar to wear important jewelry. My wedding ring, my engagement ring, and otherwise just a little costume jewelry, and I had all of that on me."

"Money?"

"Not much, and that and my credit cards are in my purse."

She stopped short and looked around for her purse. One of the women who had been doing the picking up handed it to her. Unlike the suitcases, it was not gaping open. She opened it and checked through its contents.

"Anything missing?" Mulligan asked.

"No. I don't think it was even opened. Everything's exactly as I keep it."

"Of course it wasn't touched," Culver said. "There wouldn't have been time. Mrs. Smith says she opened the door and saw at once that she'd had a burglar. She started screaming and the young ruffian knocked her out before she could get to see him. But she'd already screamed. All of us were tearing up here to come to her assistance. He had no time for even snatching her purse, much less stopping to go through it. We would have caught him in here if he had stopped for anything at all."

He was still pushing his guttersnipe-scholar line, but that took nothing away from the rightness of his thinking about the question of the tight timing. Nobody was about to give him an argument on that.

I wasn't even giving it much thought. My mind was on that box of powder. Everybody has heard about money or jewelry being hidden at the bottom of just such a box of talcum, but it seemed to me that it's done—if it ever is done—for purposes of smuggling. I was asking myself what anyone could have hoped to find at the bottom of that powder box. Certainly it couldn't enter any sane mind that a woman carrying anything she had any notion of using would undertake such a messy business as stowing it there only to face the even messier process of taking it out of there.

I made a big try at thinking with a burglar's head, and I just couldn't imagine anyone silly enough to have thought he might find anything buried in the talcum powder. I could picture a burglar who, in his disappointment at finding nothing he considered to be worth stealing, might go nastily destructive, indulging himself in a bout of vandalism. That seemed to be a possibility, but I couldn't make it stick.

I looked at all those delicate silk pretties the helpful women were gathering up off the floor. They were smoothing the things and folding them neatly. I saw nothing ripped and nothing messed up. Wouldn't an enraged vandal have ripped some of those fripperies to shreds?

Alberta Smith was helped down the stairs and out through the Quad to a car that would take her to the infirmary. Wives and classmates, even classmates well along in drink, behaved themselves. They stepped back, leaving a cleared path between the entry and that one arch- way in the Quad that campus security had left open for our comings and goings. Nobody was out of line but the one young twerp—the ubiquitous Rick Dowling, complete with camera. He popped up in our path and backed along ahead of us to take some quick shots of the walking wounded.

Larry gave me a signal, but I didn't need it. I was already moving in. I grabbed the kid by the scruff of the neck and looked for an open spot where I could throw him. I saw none, but I spotted Bob. He was standing by with his hands out. The young bastard was kicking and squirming, but with my free hand I got a good grip on the seat of his pants. Lifting him off his feet, I lateraled him off to Bob. Good old Bob, still as much man as he'd ever been, fielded my lateral neatly and dumped Mr. Dowling on the grass, sitting him down hard.

We moved on out of the archway. Culver Hoyt had volunteered his car. He had the job for it, one of those mammoth Lincolns. They build them for the guys who al- ways wanted to drive a truck but find themselves barred from that lifelong ambition by being too rich for it. Culver drove with the dean in the front seat beside him. Larry and I were in back with Alberta.

By that time she was protesting that she was all right. She didn't need all the solicitude we were pouring on her, even though it was sweet of us to do it. She was spoiling our reunion for us and she hated doing that. She'd always prided herself on being a woman who didn't spoil parties. She was going to have a lovely bed in the infirmary and she would rest and she would be fine. We were not to trouble about her any more. She wanted us to go back to the Quad and have our fun.

"I know what reunions mean to you boys," she said. "Jim and I used to come every year. We never missed one. They were the event of the year for my Jim."

I was thinking that Jim Smith must have had a lot of thin years, but I wasn't saying anything. At the infirmary Larry and Culver and the dean went upstairs with her. I stayed down in the waiting room. I wasn't a medic and, unlike Dean Mulligan, I had no official responsibility. I expected that Larry and Culver would stay long enough to see the lady settled in and that the dean would be the first of them to come back downstairs. I was waiting for him, looking for a moment of private talk.

I didn't have a long wait, but it wasn't the dean who came down. It was Larry and Culver. I asked about the dean. They were surprised that I hadn't seen him. He had been upstairs only long enough to make certain that the infirmary had a proper room for Alberta Smith and then he had taken off, leaving it to my medical buddies to see her properly installed.

I went to the reception desk and asked there if Dean Mulligan was still in the building. He wasn't. He'd gone out by the back door. My memory of campus geography was good enough for me to know that from the back door there would be a shortcut he could have taken to the dean's house. It wasn't necessary to think he had deliberately dodged the moment of private talk with me. On the other hand this wasn't the first time I'd been hit with an unnecessary thought that just wouldn't come unstuck from my mind.

Because we couldn't find any polite way of leaving him, we rode back to the Quad with Culver. He talked all the way, never shut up for a moment. It was the same thing again and again. The old place had opened itself up to the wrong class of kids. They were taking them out of public high schools. They were taking slum kids. No family background. No home discipline. He knew of alumni sons who had been turned down for admission just because at school they hadn't been in the top ten academically.

"They're turning away good boys from good families and taking in young toughs and setting up classes in remedial reading for them," he said.

My mind jumped back to the classes in remedial organic chemistry this latter-day snob had had from Larry, but I gave that the skip. Instead I made some cracks about rich kids sent to the best schools and too spoiled and lazy to make the grade against poor kids who would work their asses off to make it.

All that got me was: "Blood will tell."

I didn't know which was the more objectionable of the two Dr. Culver Hoyts—his Neil Neecey manifestation or this to-the-manor-born crap. I couldn't like either of them.

Back at the Quad he ran into a parking problem. While he had been off to the infirmary, some guy had slipped his car into the slot Culver had been using. He dropped us at the archway and went off to cruise the campus for another parking place. It was the first chance Larry and I had for putting our heads together.

"What do you think?" I asked.

"I don't know what to think," Larry said. "Somebody's crazy."

"Maybe," I said, "if you're thinking crazy with fear. Somebody's in a spot and he's stopping at nothing to get himself out of it. He killed Sooey, but he's still not in the clear."

"Yes. He thought Sooey's things were still in the room. He was up there trying to snag something she had. He had to find it and get rid of it because, when it is found, it will give him away."

"Exactly."

"But what?" Larry said. "Okay. Some idiot had his thing with her back when we were all of us lining up for it. He'd rather his wife didn't know, but what if she does find out? Has he been making her think he was a virgin when he came to the bridal bed? Even so, it was all a long time ago and what can it do to him now? She'll get mad at him? They'll quarrel about it? A man kills for that?"

"Ham Roberts didn't want his Glad to know," I said, "but Sooey made it pretty plain. I'm guessing that Glad and Ham had a do about it. That's likely why he hung the mouse on her."

"Very likely," Larry said. "But wouldn't that have been fat already in the fire? Sooey had already given him away. It was too late to shut her up and, even if it hadn't been too late, it would have been a mighty thin reason for killing a woman. Maybe you can go all out and say in a sudden burst of rage, but it wasn't that kind of killing. Too much preparation and too much calculation. This was done for a reason."

"And for a reason he's trying to search through her stuff," I said.

"That's right. Searching for what? A love letter he had written her way back then?"

"Would it need to have been way back then?" I asked. "Just because for us it was kid stuff and long since over and done with doesn't mean that for one of the boys it can't have been a continuing relationship. How about a letter written after the guy was married?"

Larry chewed that over.

"Not a record of something that happened before he

ever knew his wife," he said, "but a record of infidelity? Even so, does a guy kill for that?"

"If he has a wife who's likely to divorce him," I said, trying it for size.

Larry didn't go for the fit.

"Still too thin," he said.

"I'm wondering whether it was in oil that Ham Roberts made it so big," I said. "If he married all that loot . . ."

"A woman buys herself a husband and then holds still for it when she finds she's bought a wife beater?"

"It's been known to happen," I said. "She'll take the poke in the eye but she won't take his playing around with another woman."

Larry grinned at me.

"Since we're a couple of bachelors," he said, "we're experts on the easy answers to how a wife's mind works."

"We have the cool, objective view," I said, "untarnished by experience."

"Want to run it past Slammer for her opinion?" Larry asked.

It seemed a good suggestion. I was thinking of both Slammer and Bob—Slammer for the woman's slant as seen by a wife with a good head on her, and Bob because he'd always been sharp on what made people tick. He'll tell you he learned that from the Greeks. There was nothing human that his ancient Greeks hadn't explored.

We went into the Quad to look for them. It was some time before we could break them away. They were tied up with people and we got tied up along with them. Just about everyone in the place was buttonholing us. Everyone wanted the latest word on how Alberta Smith was doing. She appeared to be a great favorite with the regulars who had been coming back every year. Over the years when she and Jim had never missed a class party, she had herself been one of the regulars, and she had made a lot of good friends. With all those people genuinely concerned about her, it wasn't possible to give any of them a quick brush-off.

There was also Florence Hoyt. When Culver had gone off to the infirmary, Florence had attached herself to Slammer and Bob. That, I suppose, was an inevitable by-product of their room swap. It made her feel closer to them than to any of the other classmates. It seemed to me that we were going to have to wait until Culver returned from his hunt for a parking place before we could hope to break Slammer and Bob out of there. It seemed obvious that as long as Florence Hoyt was on her own, where they went she was going to go, and Dean Mulligan had asked us to keep our thinking to ourselves.

As it turned out, however, we didn't have to wait for Culver. Ham Roberts came walking into the Quad. His Glad was nowhere in evidence. At sight of Ham, Florence Hoyt wanted out. She was not in the market for any con-frontations. She excused herself hastily and took off to their room. We grabbed the opportunity and pulled Slammer and Bob away.

I had Baby parked right outside the archway. The four of us piled into the Porsche and I ran us down to the lake. Down there I headed for a nice, quiet spot where we could park and talk. There had been a time when I had taken girls there. Larry and I filled the Careys in on our thinking. Among the four of us we kicked it around.

"Jealous of a wild oat buried in antiquity?" Slammer said. "It would need to be the world's stupidest woman."

"That it would," Bob said, "but how could you describe

Glad Roberts more precisely? Even the unspeakable Ham could have married her only for her money."

"She's pretty," Slammer said, "and if you took away the rocks, she could be sexy. I would guess she doesn't wear them to bed."

"Want to bet?" Larry said.

"So she's jealous and they quarreled." Bob summed it up. "Ham pasted her in the eye. Before he killed Sooey or after, and what could Sooey have that he would now be trying to find?"

We tried the love-letter thought on them, something more recent than the antique wild oat. Slammer called it possible. Bob said no.

"I can't see Ham as a letter writer," he said. "It has to be something else."

"Like what?" Larry asked.

None of them had any ideas. I came up with the far-out one.

"Jewelry," I said, "a piece of jewelry. Let's say it was Glad's. It disappeared. Ham convinced her that she must have lost it somewhere, but actually he'd swiped it and given it to Sooey. Now there's something that would hit Glad where she lives."

"Matthew, my love," Slammer said, "you're reaching."

I worked at defending it. I suppose I was trying to convince myself.

"There's his tigers-in-the-bar story," I said. "Was that just plain bad taste, or did he tell it for Glad's benefit? It could have been a way of demonstrating to her that he felt nothing for Sooey."

Bob shook his head.

"We know Ham. That's much too subtle for him," he

said. "This is one stupid guy. You have him thinking with your kind of mind, Matt, and that he hasn't got."

"Anyhow," Larry said, "we're fixing on Ham and that's no good. It could be almost anyone."

"Almost anyone in the good old class," Bob said.

"Right," I agreed. "She came with the idea of pulling something off. She had something on somebody and she was going to put it to him. She was being the good old party girl, everybody's pal, not a thought in her head, and all the time she was working hard at staying sober. She hadn't come for any merry booze-up. She had business to do."

"There's an easy way to clear the whole thing up," Slammer said.

"How?"

"The police go through her things and find what her killer was looking for," she said. "It has to be something that will point to him."

"Do you think they will?" Larry asked. "Go through her things, I mean. They don't want to think murder."

"And the dean?" Bob said. "Her things are locked up in his office."

"He doesn't want to think murder either," Larry said.

I headed to where I'd parked Baby.

"It's up to us to make him think," I said.

We drove back to the Quad. Of course my handy parking spot was gone. I offered to drop the others while I went looking for a new place to leave the Porsche, but they elected to ride around with me. It didn't take much riding. There were empty spaces alongside the next dorm. We left her and the four of us walked across campus to the dean's house. It was completely dark, not a light showing at any window. I looked at my watch. Midnight had been and gone.

"Does he live alone in all that house?" Slammer asked.

We told her about the wife and kids.

"Then you can't go rousing them at this time of night," she said. "Be civilized."

"I can't believe he's asleep," I said.

"I can believe his children are," Slammer told me. "We spoiled ours when they were small but they were always in bed and asleep long before midnight."

Bob took a hand. "If you were the dean," he said, "where would you be now?"

"At my reunion," Larry said. "We should have asked him what class he was."

"If I were the dean," I said, "I would be in my office doing a search of Sooey's luggage."

"Do you suppose he might be?" Bob asked.

"Not a chance," I said. "He isn't me."

"Do you know where his office is?" Slammer asked.

We knew where the dean's office used to be. We each had memories of uncomfortable sessions we'd had in that room with his predecessor of our era.

We went over there. The door was locked, and it wasn't like a dorm-room door. It was solid and it had a good lock on it. There were scratches and dents in it that shouldn't have been there. Someone had been working on that lock.

"Oho," Bob said. "Attempted burglary."

"Unless it was more than attempted," I said.

"How more?"

"Like successful."

"With the door locked?"

"It could have been worked on and opened," I said. "A

locked door is only a locked door. It isn't necessarily one that hasn't been opened."

"You're just looking for an excuse to disturb the sleep of the dean's little ones," Slammer said.

I had a better idea than that. We went looking for a campus cop. We found one, of course, standing guard on the entrance of the nearest reunion headquarters. I reported to him that someone had tampered with the lock on the door of the dean's office.

"It looks like Dean Mulligan has had a burglar," I said.

There were two of them on the entrance and he left it to his partner to hold it down alone. Taking it at a trot, he led us back to the Administration Building. Inside, however he went the wrong way. We tried to set him straight but he wasn't listening. He knew where the dean's office was.

At the door of his choosing, he turned on us.

"Nobody's been working on this door," he said. "No dents. No scratches." He supposed that we thought we were being very funny, but he would have hoped that we were old enough to know better. He suggested that we go back to our reunion and behave ourselves.

We persuaded him to come down the corridor to that other door.

"There's nothing down there but secretaries," he said.

So it was only the door of a secretary's office that had been worked on and obviously by someone of our vintage who, like us, unaware of changes, had made our mistake.

CHAPTER 5

It may have been a load off our minds, but the campus cop
took a broader view. Breaking and entering was breaking
and entering and he had a democratic attitude toward
doors. In his eyes all doors were equal. He brought out a
master key and unlocked the door to that secretarial office.
Inside everything was neat. He checked file cabinets and
desk drawers. Such telltale marks of tampering as we had
seen on the office door were nowhere to be found inside
the office.

"Looks like he just tried," the cop said. "Looks like he
didn't get in."

"Or if he did," Bob said, "he saw immediately that he
was in the wrong place and he backed right out again without touching anything."

There could be no question but that Bob had the right
of it. None of us was prepared to give the cop any part of
what we were thinking. All of that had to be saved for
Dean Mulligan, but the burglar we had in mind would
have known at first sight that what he had entered was no
longer the dean's office.

The old room we remembered had been cut up with par-
titions to make a series of cubicles for the secretaries. No
dean could be expected to function in one of those little
cubbyholes. He would need quarters impressive enough to
strike awe in the breast of an errant undergraduate.

Our putative burglar, furthermore, would not have been looking for something locked away in a desk drawer or in a file. He would have been looking for a set of lady's luggage and for something stowed away in one of those pieces. Even if he could have been so dim that he would not recognize that on dimensions alone the cubbyholes were not deanish, he would have seen at once that he was in the wrong place for what he wanted.

I would very much have liked to ask our cop to use that master key of his to give us a look inside Dean Mulligan's office, but that was clearly not the kind of thing that could be asked of a cop. It was going to have to wait till morning when we could take it up with the dean himself.

We pulled out of the Administration Building and returned to the Quad. It had seemed to me when we had stopped by there earlier that every last classmate, every last wife, and every last widow had flocked around to ask us how Alberta Smith was doing. Not so. At least one had missed. She was another of the widows. Her name was Jane Struthers. I remembered her late husband well. He had been the big gun in our defensive line, two hundred thirty pounds of sheer destruction.

Off the field you could never have imagined it of him. Inside that mountain of muscle there was a brain, but apart from that nothing but cream puff, the sweetest, gentlest, and kindest Goliath you could ever hope to know. Hobie Struthers had been one of our best buddies. I'd heard of his death from Larry. Hobie had gone the way the big ones all too often go, the mid-life coronary.

So now Jane buttonholed us.

"I feel as though I know the three of you," she said. "Hobie talked of you so much. He always said the best thing he got out of his four years here was knowing Bob and Larry and Matt."

"When we knew him, he had better judgment," Bob said.

"No, seriously. I'm frightened. I have to talk to someone and I'd like to talk to you three. If Hobie were here, he would be talking to you."

"Frightened?" I asked. "Of what?"

"I don't know. I came here expecting to room with Alberta. She and I are friends from way back. We were at school together and we were together at Smith. It's really been a lifelong friendship. Hobie and Jim Smith hadn't been at all close when they were here. That came about later, really through Alberta and me."

"What happened on the room deal then?" Larry asked.

"It was Amanda. She asked Alberta if they couldn't go in together, and Alberta couldn't possibly say no. I didn't want her to, as a matter of fact. I love being with Alberta, of course, but it didn't mean that I wasn't seeing a lot of her anyhow and it was obvious that I'd be all right while this was likely to be difficult and uncomfortable for Amanda. She was the one who needed a good friend with her, and they were good friends."

"Difficult and uncomfortable" seemed to be words that were grossly inadequate for what Sooey had found at reunion.

"Why did she have such a special need for a friend?" Bob asked. "She may not have known all of us, but there couldn't have been many she didn't know."

He caught a scowl from Slammer. Even without it I don't think he would have made it any more explicit.

"I don't know," Jane said. "She'd never come back before. She never came with Graystock."

"I've never been before," Slammer said.

"Oh, but that's different. You're with Bob, but, more than that, Amanda's situation was special."

"How special?" I asked.

"Just special. I never gossiped about her when she was alive. I certainly shan't start now."

"Even if it may be saying something about how she died?" Larry asked.

Even though we might have had our own ideas of what had been special about Sooey's situation, it seemed most unlikely that Jane Struthers would have been aware of that part of Amanda Graystock's history. I could understand why Larry should have been pushing for an answer.

His question made Jane jump.

"Then you know," she said.

"We know a great deal and we suspect a lot more," Larry said.

"She was murdered. She didn't just die." Jane brought the words out in a panicky rush. "I knew her. She drank, possibly even too much, but sedatives? She never took anything like that. She wasn't the type. She was too placid and too cheerful for it. She never needed anything. I couldn't believe it was suicide or accident or anything like that, but I kept telling myself it must have been, but now with what happened to Alberta . . . She was Amanda's friend and I was Amanda's friend. It's crazy, but I can't pretend I'm not scared. Is it to be Amanda and all her friends?"

"He wasn't after Alberta," Slammer said. "He was after Amanda's luggage."

"But it wasn't in the room. It had been taken away."

"Exactly, and when he discovered that," I said, "he tried to go where her things had been taken and get at them there. He didn't succeed, but it's that he's after, not a flock of you widows."

We told her where we had just been with the campus cop.

"So anything you know about her might be a help toward clearing this thing up. It has to be that there was something between her and one of the men back to this reunion." Larry was pushing it again. "Amanda was trying something on with him. We hate to think it, but it looks like blackmail. He killed her, and now he's after something she had that would be evidence against him. It will be a letter or something of that sort."

"Blackmail?" Jane was shaking her head. She couldn't believe it or she didn't want to believe it. "Amanda wouldn't have. There was nothing vicious or unkind about her. She may have had some peculiar ideas, but even that—it's become acceptable. Young people are doing it, daughters and sons of one's friends—young people from the nicest families. It really comes down to nothing much more than that she was before her time."

"Promiscuity," Slammer said. "It wasn't invented yesterday. It isn't something that has just begun, a fresh way of life unknown when we were kids."

"Promiscuity?" Jane said. "No. I can swear for her there. She was absolutely faithful to Graystock. We used to say . . ." She broke off and took a long breath. "But never mind that," she said. "It was nobody's business and nothing anyone would kill her for."

She couldn't go that far and then not give us the rest of it. She had said that it wasn't anything so impossibly scandalous. In fact it was something that had become respectable. That made it something she didn't need to be so reluctant to repeat. Her certainty that it could have no possible relevance to Sooey's murder and the assault on Alberta Smith wasn't convincing us. There could always be a connection that she wasn't seeing. I was inclined to think that she was probably too nice-minded to see it. I told her as much.

"We will probably see a connection you're missing," I said. "We're not at all nice-minded."

For what seemed like a very long time she hesitated. She was clearly at the brink of speaking out but, having come to the brink, she was shrinking back.

"You would have had no hesitation about telling Hobie what you're thinking," Bob said.

"Oh, Hobie knew. Actually he told me."

"He would have told us," I said. "We always shared everything."

"Oh, well," she said. "Amanda wasn't a widow. Coming to reunion as a widow, it might have been difficult for her."

I could make no sense of that.

"Divorced?" I asked.

I couldn't believe it. That the class kept in touch with widows was one thing. Treating divorcees as widows seemed most peculiarly excessive.

"Nonsense," Bob said. "Graystock died. I know he died. There was the obituary, memorial gifts, the lot."

"Of course she was a widow," Larry said.

"It comes to the same thing," Jane said, "but strictly speaking, she wasn't."

"Strictly speaking is all very well," Bob said, "but couldn't you just make it lucidly as well."

"They were never married," Jane said. "They just cohabited. They didn't believe in marriage, except that it always seemed to me that it was she who didn't believe in it. He just went along since it really made no difference. No license and no ceremony, but otherwise they were just like any other happily married couple. I know many couples who did all the legal and religious things and live in unending misery, even hating each other."

She had me completely knocked over. I could think of nothing I could have called more completely unlike Sooey Generous. Though unsanctified bedplay had never been foreign to her, that she should have made it a matter of principled conviction struck me as totally out of character for her. Careless and carefree she had always been, but sternly and rigidly principled? This was in no way the Sooey Generous I had known, and nobody could tell me I hadn't known her well.

"But she called herself Mrs. Graystock, didn't she?" Slammer asked.

Jane Struthers answered that and answered it in full. Although it had been done as a matter of principle just as many young people were doing it in this latter day, there had been that difference. The new generation was flaunting it. Our generation—and Sooey had been of our generation —didn't go that far.

"Yes," Bob said. "I can understand that, even though I can't understand her doing it. I would have said it was out of character for her."

His thinking was clearly running along the same lines as mine. Slammer concurred with him, or at least with his understanding. She hadn't known Sooey as we had. It was natural that she shouldn't have been sharing our reservations.

"That would be the difference," Slammer said. "We in our time were brought up to put a high value on privacy. A thing like that would be most private, their business and theirs alone. What we valued as privacy the young people of today would call hypocrisy."

"Of the two of them," Jane said, "it was Graystock who felt that way. She told people. She told Alberta. She told me, even though she had no idea that I'd already known it from Hobie. It embarrassed Graystock to have her telling it, but she made no more secret of it than the kids do today. She wanted people to know."

"But now, when he's dead, she comes to reunion calling herself Mrs. Graystock," I said.

Jane shrugged.

"She wanted to come. She would hardly have been welcome any other way. She would have been an embarrassment to the committee. I suppose she didn't want that."

"A minor embarrassment to them," I said. "Nothing to the embarrassment she'll have caused them before this thing is finished."

"Oh, come," Jane said. "After all, she came to have a good time. She didn't come to get herself murdered."

"She came to play some kind of dangerous game," I said. "It backfired on her, and it's left her dead."

"What dangerous game?"

"The best guess seems to be blackmail," Slammer told her.

"But who? With what?"

"Some member of the illustrious class," Slammer said, "and with whatever it may be he wants to find in her luggage before someone else finds it and it hangs him."

"It must be something very nasty," Jane said.

"Certainly something dangerous."

That was Larry, and he might have done better not saying it. Jane Struthers turned white. Her lips quivered. I looked at her hands. They had begun to shake.

"Something secret," she said. "Something he can't have known before this. We were her friends, Alberta and I. She confided in us. All sorts of people know how close we were. If he's thinking that we might know, that she might have told us . . ."

Her voice trailed off into silence. She was much too frightened to finish what she had started to say. None of us was inclined to finish it for her, but we knew what she was thinking.

Larry took hold.

"The mayor and the police," he said, "don't want to call it murder, and the administration people here on campus are not at all inclined to push them. They're all mired down in their wishful thinking. A woman murdered at reunion and murdered by an alumnus—they don't want the scandal."

"Don't be too hard on them," Slammer said. "You wouldn't in their place."

"Somebody has to push," Jane Struthers said. "We have to push them."

"First thing in the morning." I was making her the promise but, even more than that, I was making it to myself. "We have the lever we can use to move them. Someone's been trying to get at her luggage. We'll insist on someone going through it—town police, campus security people, Dean Mulligan, someone in authority. They'll find whatever it is the killer is after, and that will finish it. It will clear the whole thing up."

It seemed simple enough. It even seemed inevitable. I had set myself to think with the killer's mind, and I had the delusion that I was doing a right good job of it. I like to believe that there was nothing wrong with my thinking and that the defect lay only in the mind that I was using. Perhaps I should have recognized that the killer was an active type but that in the mentality department he had nothing great to go along with.

Come morning, the five of us were camped on Dean Mulligan's doorstep. Jane Struthers had become a part of our little closed circle. That was no more than proper, and it was proper every which way. If Hobie had been there, he would have been one of us from the first, and she would have been right in there with him every bit as much as Slammer was with Bob. In addition to being Hobie's widow, however, Jane had a ticket of admission in her own right. She alone was with the four of us in crying murder.

So when Danny Mulligan came to work, he found our quintet of supersleuths there before him. He asked us to come in and, seeing that there were enough chairs and that we would find them comfortable, he worked hard at creating the air of jovial bonhomie suitable for fellow alumni well met in a time of foolish festivity.

"Having a good reunion?" he asked.

"Good enough for an event that's more than a little loused up with murder," Larry said.

Dean Mulligan chuckled, and he wasn't putting it on. It was an authentically mirthful chuckle.

"According to the police chief," he said, "you guys are adding two and two and getting five."

"And that's something he might be doing himself," Bob said, "if it wasn't that he's never learned to count past four."

"Oh, come on, gang!" Dean Danny said. "Mrs. Graystock died and then later a sneak thief happened to hit the room she had been occupying. You are not prepared to ac-

cept that as a coincidence. I agree. It may very well not
have been a coincidence. Mrs. Smith, naturally upset by
the sudden death of her friend, may very well not have had
a mind for remembering to lock her door when she left her
room. I can well imagine how it could have been the one
room most accessible to a burglar."

"If you work hard enough at explaining everything
away," I said.

"To give it any greater significance," the dean said, "is
what we here in academia call *post hoc propter hoc* reasoning. Just because Event B has followed Event A in time
doesn't necessarily mean that A is the cause of B."

"Professor Carey also hangs out in academia," Slammer
said, "and I am his wife. If we are going to toss the learned
Latin around, I'll contribute *argumentum ad hominem*.
We all belong to this great and glorious university family.
In our illustrious numbers there cannot possibly be a
killer."

"Not impossible," the dean said, "but I am finding it
hard to believe."

"Will it help you," Bob said, "if we recognize that the
old place has improved greatly since our day? By the time
you came along the nobility level had risen so high that
there may be no contemporary of yours who cannot be
considered above suspicion. We would like to think as well
of our contemporaries, but the evidence rules it out. The
killer has established himself as being of no recent vintage."

"Our new evidence pins that down," I said.

"What new evidence?"

"If you haven't yet heard, there was an attempted break-
in in one of the offices over here last night."

"I have heard," the dean said. "It was reported to me.

The attempt was unsuccessful and it was clearly done by an outsider, someone with absolutely no knowledge of this building. Of all the offices here, certainly that one would be the least promising for any burglar. It is the door to the typists' pool."

"And so it is," I said. "Think back to when you were an undergraduate. Did you ever have any business that took you through that door?"

"No, I didn't. Of course I didn't."

"We did."

"So you dated some of the typists."

Despite his best efforts to be patient with us, a note of weariness crept into his tone. We had already briefed him on Sooey Generous. He was bracing himself to hear further revelations of the extent of our youthful amatory exploits. He was all too evidently casting about in his mind for a way to chop us off before we could do our boasting in the presence of the ladies.

"No," I said. "In our day that was the door to the dean's office. His furniture was less comfortable than this, but they gave him more space. I remember walking the last mile from the door to his desk. Obviously between our time and yours the offices were changed around and the old dean's office was partitioned off into the cubicles for the typists."

Danny Mulligan thought about that for a moment or two. It wasn't that he was such a slow study; but, forced out of what he'd thought was his eminently reasonable position, he now had considerable reordering to do on his thinking.

"He thought he would be breaking in here?" he said.

"And since he was of our vintage," I said, "he worked on

the wrong door. For one of us it was the most natural mistake."

"But my office? Why my office?"

"Because in the hearing of a whole roomful of our crowd you announced that all of Mrs. Graystock's things had been packed up and locked away in your office."

Dean Danny began to sweat.

"I did do that, didn't I?" he said.

"You did." I had him reeling and I was going to hammer all my points home before he could recover his equilibrium. "You must see," I said, "that it pins a couple of things down. First it tells us that our man was a student here back in the time before the dean's office was moved. It also tells us that the burglary was directed against Mrs. Graystock's things. Furthermore, since there was nobody around but our classmates when you announced that her things were locked up in your office, we can pin it down closer than just somebody who was here before the offices were moved. We can say with pretty good certainty that our man is a member of our great and glorious class."

The dean sighed.

"I'll grant you all that," he said, "but still it's insane. What can the man be after?"

"Something she had," Bob said, "and she died of having it. It must be something he couldn't have had her showing about, something she was using for blackmailing him."

"So now," Dean Danny said, "she can't blackmail him, but this thing, whatever it may be, if found among her stuff, can still ruin him."

He had come most of the way. Larry moved in to give it another little push.

"Now more than ever," he said. "Because now it will identify him as her murderer."

The dean hauled out his handkerchief and mopped his face. He couldn't have been sweating more if he had himself been the suspect.

Jane Struthers chose that moment to speak, and I could have wished she hadn't.

"This is all very well," she said, "but it just isn't possible that Amanda could have been blackmailing anyone. I knew her well. We were friends. It just wasn't in her to do anything like that. There never was a kinder woman. She was generosity itself."

The generosity touch was unfortunate. I tried to put it from my mind. I could see that Larry and Bob were engaged in a similar struggle. It didn't help that Slammer, although she was saying nothing, was regarding us with a look I can describe only as quizzical.

Larry stepped into it.

"You knew her well," he said. "How was she fixed for money? Were you and she close enough? Do you know about that?"

"She was very badly off," Jane said. "She couldn't manage on income and she was eating into principal, but she wasn't desperate about it or anything like that. In fact she was taking it too blithely. It worried me, I know. But she would just say airily that sometime soon she was going to have to find a job or do something."

"Or do something," Dean Danny echoed the words. On his lips they came out as a groan.

"Had she ever had any work experience?" Slammer asked. "Find a job? Did she have any marketable skills?"

"No, she didn't. That was what was so worrying. She just didn't seem to recognize that there might be a problem about getting a job. A woman of her age with no experience and no training."

"You talked to her about it?" Larry asked.

"Several times, but all she'd say was that she would find a way. She always had. There was no reason to think anything but that she always would."

"And no hint of what the way would be?" the dean asked.

"I never thought that she knew herself. She was always so vague."

The question was inevitable. I left it unspoken but that didn't mean that it hadn't jumped into my mind. It seemed to me that Jane Struthers was alone in not confronting it. Although nobody was putting it into words, I was convinced that all of us, with only the possible exception of Jane, had to be thinking it. Had she been so vague about the way she would find because vagueness had always been her way of life, or had it been that she had known precisely what the way was to be and that in this case it had been a vagueness specifically tailored to cover the unmentionable?

I suppose we each found an answer to that question and that the answers carried varying degrees of conviction. Jane Struthers, who had been her friend and whose friendly contacts with her had been recent, was simply unable to believe that jolly, open Amanda, firmly embedded in her attitude of live-and-let-live, could ever have brought herself to do anything devious or could ever have summoned up the toughness it would have taken to drive a man into a corner from which he could find no exit short of murder.

I can guess that Larry and Bob were, like me, not too far from Jane in the difficulty we were having with believing what seemed to be the obvious. We, the three of us, had also been her friends. You may be thinking that "friend" is a word insufficient to the facts; but, nevertheless, whatever else there had been between Sooey and the three of us, there had been friendship as well. We had called her Generous and, even though the naming might have been specific, we were none of us unaware of its broader implications. We remembered her as a generous spirit.

I can speak for the argument I was waging with myself. In the face of all the indications I found myself unable to conceive of Sooey as a blackmailer. She was too gentle and too easy-going. I tried to tell myself that the days when I had known her were long in the past. Through the intervening years she'd been doing a lot of living and doesn't living toughen us all?

It was all very well to say that she had never been devious and that she was incapable of duplicity. We'd had it demonstrated to us that in the years since we had known her this much she had learned. There was the trick she had been playing with her drinks. In the way she'd handled that she had given every evidence of practiced skill. Certainly there we'd had a glimpse of something that wasn't the old Sooey of our youthful memories.

Taking all that into consideration, I was still experiencing great difficulty in shaping up any credible picture of the moment. Sooey confronting a man with an ultimatum? Sooey presenting a threat? Even as I was telling myself that I couldn't picture it, I found myself indeed picturing it.

Hard as it might have been to imagine her doing it, it was all too easy to imagine her doing it badly, plunging into it without having set up any safeguards. Certainly that had been like her. If she was going to blackmail a man, it would have been done from the friendliest sort of approach, cozily over a drink. There had been a drink. We could have no doubt of that.

For obvious reasons the two who were most free of any

doubt were Slammer and the newest convert, Dean Daniel Mulligan. It was natural enough. Neither of them had been her friend. They were not burdened with any long-held image of her. They didn't have to put themselves through any painful process of revision.

We had made our point. The dean was at last ready to move, but he was only mentally ready. Action was going to have to wait. He couldn't act unless officially, and official action demanded all the official preliminaries.

The great Abner Dale, president of the university, had to be informed. The mayor and the police chief, despite their previously displayed lack of interest, had to be brought back into the act.

The high-powered attorney who was counsel to the university had to be consulted. There was also a potentially troublesome problem of Sooey's next of kin. Inquiries up to that point had indicated that there were none, and Jane Struthers was certain that with Graystock's death Amanda had been left alone in the world without even as much as some remote cousin to survive her. The dean, nevertheless, was determined that we were not going to be turned loose to go pawing through her things. There would be a search. He assured us of that. It could be done, however, only by accredited officialdom and in the most formally official manner.

"I should be able to set it up for you people to be present to witness it," he said.

We thanked him for that.

"Maybe I don't have to tell you this," I said, "but you'll also have to set it up so that nobody can possibly get at her stuff before it's searched."

He came up from behind his desk and fished a key ring out of his pocket. Unlocking a door behind his desk, he opened it to a large closet. It was a well-filled closet and the least of what it contained was an AG-monogrammed suitcase. Although we were all focused on the suitcase, some of the rest of what he had in there couldn't escape our notice. That closet looked like a well-stocked head shop.

"Confiscated items held as evidence pending disciplinary hearings," Dean Danny said.

Maybe he wanted to let us know that a dean's life was not a simple one. He had other problems. None of us, however, was interested in picking up on that.

"Is that all she had?" Slammer asked. "Just the one bag?"

It was a question that wouldn't have occurred to me. For the four days and some of reunion I had packed all I was going to need in just one bag and Larry had come no more heavily laden. We had, however, helped with the luggage when the Careys switched rooms with the Hoyts. In each room there had been a sizable mound of luggage to be shifted. It was one of the obvious differences between men and women.

Even as I was beginning to think that Dean Danny had slipped up, Jane Struthers supplied the answer.

"She hadn't been planning on staying the whole time," Jane said. "It was going to be just the one night, long enough to see everybody and that's all."

For me that translated into just long enough to accomplish what she had come to do and then no lingering on at the scene of the crime. Poor Sooey—she hadn't even had the whole of her one night.

It was a couple of hours before Dean Mulligan had all his official preliminaries out of the way. His message came to us at lunch. We were to meet in his office at two o'clock.

Everyone was there—university president, university counsel, the mayor, the police chief. Everything was done with the most exaggerated regard for legality and formal ceremony. Dean Mulligan produced Sooey's keys and, setting the case on his cleared desk top, he unlocked it.

He had to sort the luggage key out from the others on the key ring. They seemed the usual assortment—car keys, house keys, and such. There was one key that evidently didn't fit the key ring. It wasn't secured to the ring in the usual way. It was fastened to it with a wrapping of tape. It made for some clumsiness in the handling of the luggage key. Seeing it, I came near to choking up. It brought Sooey most particularly close to me. It was so typical of the way she had always done things, always by some fumbling improvisation. I couldn't move away from the thought that such was the way she died. She had come to it by way of a fumbling improvisation.

Mulligan took great pains to make his every move in full view of each of the assembled witnesses. I found myself waiting for the moment when he would say: "I have nothing up my sleeve."

With the same ostentatious care he unpacked the case, removing its contents item by item and examining each piece before setting it aside. I'm not going to burden you with the catalog. You can have no interest in knowing just what she'd brought for her one-night stay in the way of nightdress, robe, slippers, a couple of changes of frock, and so forth.

There was a secretary present, and as each item came out, she was making a note of it. After the search had been completed, she typed up the inventory list and we all signed it.

The dean emptied the case and he even searched its lin-

ing. He came up with absolutely nothing. All there was to
be learned from the search was that Sooey had favored pale
pink underwear and that I would have known in any case if
I hadn't forgotten.

It was a setback, but I was still working at thinking with
the killer's mind.

"The guy who went through Mrs. Smith's things," I
said, "knew what he was looking for, and it was something
he thought could have been hidden away at the bottom of
a powder box."

There was a powder box sitting among the other stuff
that had been unpacked on to the dean's desk. He looked
from me to it, and his looked was pained. Squaring his
shoulders and setting his jaw, he performed heroically.

There was a large ashtray on the desk. Operating with
the greatest possible care, he worked at transferring the
powder from box to ashtray. The powder expanded at
every touch. For all his care, it just couldn't be confined. It
took off in clouds only to settle back on the dean, dusting
his hair and his hands and his clothes.

The ashtray that had seemed far more capacious than
the powder box proved to be grossly insufficient. The
powder piled up. It drifted all over the desk. Dean Danny,
nevertheless, doggedly worked his way down to the bottom
of the box. He turned to me. Displaying its emptiness to
all of the assembled witnesses, he reserved the first look for
me.

I felt that I owed him an apology. I didn't know precisely what I would be apologizing for, unless it might be
the killer's mind.

CHAPTER 6

Nobody should have been happy with the result, but in defiance of all logic, there were those who seemed to be liking it very much. Neither the mayor nor the police chief was saying: "I told you so," but there was nothing in their demeanor that wasn't shouting it. They were obnoxiously smug. They had indulged the amateurs in their wild fancies and now they were going back to the serious business of running the town. There would be no more distractions from the distribution of traffic tickets. It was no more than was to be expected from that pair, but from learned counsel and august president I had hoped for better.

It was a disappointment. The search of Sooey's bag had proved nothing and had fingered nobody. I could see only one possible conclusion to be drawn from our failure. The killer, convinced that she had been holding something tangible to back up the threat with which she had confronted him, had assumed that she would have brought this something to reunion with her.

I could imagine that after killing her, or even while she was deep in the drugged sleep that would have preceded death, he had searched her. The searching process might very well have been what the Peeping Tom had seen. The fact that the killer had gone on searching and had taken wild risks to do it certainly indicated that on her person he had not found this thing he feared. It followed quite naturally that he would decide that her luggage would have to be the next place to look.

So he had underestimated her and I, trying to think with his mind, had done no less. If she was holding something he had to fear, she hadn't brought it with her. She had left it in some secure place. She might even have left it in such a way that it would come to light. I was working at imagining Sooey leaving the thing with someone she trusted:

"I'm going away for a day or two. If I don't return to retrieve this from you in forty-eight hours, take it to the police."

Even to me that sounded comically melodramatic; but by reminding myself that blackmail and murder are the very stuff of melodrama, I kicked any such reservations away.

The failure of our search proved nothing more than that the killer had been mistaken in his guess on where she had been keeping the material with which she had threatened him. To take the position that this failure to find anything incriminating in the suitcase pulled all foundation out from under our theory that her death had been murder was to permit wishful thinking to unseat reason.

We had won ourselves only one convert, and that was Dean Daniel Mulligan. He had come over all the way. He was staunchly with us. He had become a true believer. None of us could understand how the other two gentlemen of the administration could persist in not seeing it our way until Slammer came up with an explanation.

"They just can't believe it of any member of the great and glorious class," she said. "Dean Danny has been seeing more than a little of you three lads. How could it be that the scales wouldn't be fallen from his eyes?"

So there it stood. We were as much convinced as ever,

but it was the consensus that we had come to the end of the road. Except for the possibility that Sooey had left hard evidence that would sometime surface somewhere to make our cry of murder stand up, this was going to be a killing that would pass off as something like accidental death by her own hand.

It was the consensus and I had no recognizable ground for not going along with it, but I was haunted by the feeling that there was some small loose end somewhere that we were overlooking. I kept searching my mind for what it might be and I could come up with nothing but the big mistake I'd made.

There was the young Peeping Tom I had kicked downstairs. It just couldn't have been a coincidence that he had done his peeping through the very keyhole beyond which lay something extraordinary to see. That kid had witnessed something at an earlier time. He had known something. When we had come on him, he hadn't been there just taking a random peep at what would have appeared to be a woman asleep in all her clothes. He had been back at the keyhole to check on something he had seen earlier. I was guessing that it would have been something like the killer's search of Sooey's body.

So there was someone who had some knowledge, and I couldn't rid myself of the thought that it would have to be precisely the knowledge we needed. We had told Dean Danny about him and, now in our time of impasse, I reminded the dean.

"I know," he said. "But he hasn't come forward to volunteer anything, and your description of him gives me nothing to go along with."

He explained that any time in the college year he would have had an idea, within some relatively broad limits, of which undergraduates might be where. But the term was over. The kids were going off on vacation. The exodus had been going on for a week or more. To a large extent departure times depended on the examination schedule. A student whose exams had come bunched at the beginning of the examination period was likely to have pulled out early, immediately after he had completed the last of his exams.

By the time reunions started, most of the students would have been gone. The senior class stayed on because they would be around for commencement, and those festivities didn't begin until immediately after the reunions folded. The kids who had jobs working the reunions also stayed, and so did the kids in the singing groups. It was a big money-making time for the singers. They did the rounds, entertaining at all the reunions, and they were well paid by the entertainment committees.

"I can work up lists of all those people," Danny said, "but it's a good bet that your boy wouldn't be among them. They're all kept much too busy."

"Not all of them," I said. "What about the seniors just waiting around for commencement?"

He shook his head.

"No," he said. "The only seniors you'll find around your reunion are the ones you have working your reunion and kids who have fathers or uncles in your class. Remember the way it was when you graduated. You hit the reunions, sure, but which? Wasn't it the first, second, and third? That was where your older contemporaries were, the guys who were your buddies, and they were now coming back. They were the people you wanted to see and to be with, partly because they were your friends and partly because they were back with the news of what it was like out there."

We kicked it around, but it always came back to the same thing. Larry and I were unable to give him a description that could do him or us any good.

"The best bet," he said, "would be that it is a boy who lives in the dorm. Instead of going home when his exams are over, he hangs on through reunion because, living in the dorm, he can't be denied access and, being there, he can freeload at your bars. They do it and we know it, but we have no way of stopping it."

"Living there and freeloading at the bars?" Larry said. "We haven't seen him since."

"You wouldn't," the dean said. "It's a good bet that he pulled out that very night to go home for the summer. If you're right—and there's every reason to think you are—he'd seen something he didn't want to get mixed up in, and then he ran afoul of the two of you. He lost his appetite for reunion. He'd soaked up all the kicks in the ass anybody could want."

I couldn't quarrel with any of that, but I couldn't be satisfied with it either. I kept asking myself why I should have been feeling so involved. Anything I'd had with Sooey had been so very long ago, but I did remember it and the memories were good. She had been kind and warm and sweet. It wasn't an old love that had never died and it wasn't an old love now renewed. Love it had never been, but it had been much liking and much affection and much fun.

I was trying to tell myself that all the indications said she had been playing an ugly game and she had been asking for it, but the answer that kept coming at me was that she was dead and only because she had been too good to know how to make a workable job of playing her nasty game.

I went looking for the lad who had broken up the Ham Roberts–Culver Hoyt fight. He was pumping beer. He got one of the other fellows to take over for him long enough to join me for a drink out of my Virginia Gentleman bottle. I tried him with the best description of the peeper that I could manage. He gave it hard thought half way down his whiskey glass and then with evident sorrow he told me he couldn't help me.

"Mr. Erridge, sir," he said.

I don't know why the young, if they have good manners, have to carry them so far as to make a man feel his age.

"Mr. Erridge, sir, you're asking the impossible. That could be any one of half the creeps on campus. The only reason it can't be one of the other half is because those are girl creeps. They all look like that. They're all engaged in the nonstop quest for a kick in the tail. It comes of the admissions people wanting a widely varied student body. It seems like they admit twelve of those to counterbalance one of me. If you ask me, they are overdoing it."

"One that lives here on the Quad?" I was still trying.

He shook his head. "No good," he said. "I'll keep thinking. If anything comes to me, I'll let you know."

It was a politeness and it was kindness. He just couldn't make it sound as though I were to expect much of it.

I would have liked to call him by name but, although he wore a name plate pinned to his T-shirt, it was nothing I could handle. The beginning of it was deceptively accessible—T-h-o-m—but beyond that it lost me in a dense Eastern European forest of Cs, Zs, and Ws so closely packed around a paucity of intervening vowels that it gave my tongue no place to go. Despite my best efforts to do it unobtrusively, he caught me in my overstudious effort to read his name plate. He grinned at me and he gave me a big wink.

"Call me Tommy," he said. "Everybody does, everybody but the Slavic language majors. They like to practice their accent. I have an uncle who changed it to Thomson, but I ask you, sir. Don't you think that's chickening out?"

"We'll make a deal," I said. "It'll be Tommy if you'll stop calling me sir."

"Deal," he said.

"And about that guy, I'll be grateful if you give it a good try," I said. "Maybe ask around just in case one of the other fellows might have an idea. I wouldn't be bothering you with it if it wasn't important."

"Right," he said. "I'll be thinking, and I'll ask around."

He went back to his beer pump. It was a time of lull in the Quad. Most of the gang had gone off somewhere. I could have looked at the program and determined whether it was the art museum or the new gym they had been taken to inspect. I could work up no interest.

At tables here and there a scattering of people remained. Apart from meal times when everyone moved indoors to feed, the Quad was never totally empty. There were always those few guys who wouldn't let an arranged program or anything else intrude on what they had come for, whether it was uninterrupted drinking or cutting up old touches with buddies too long unseen.

As I passed across the Quad one group and another urged me to come sit with them, but I wasn't of a mood to go slopping around in old memories. I was beating on my brain, trying to whack out of it what seemed to be the elusive memory of something recent. I couldn't rid myself of the feeling that there was something there—something that

I'd heard or seen or just sensed. If I could only make it surface, it would be something I should be thinking about.

I was going somewhere to think without any clear notion of where that was to be. I suppose it was instinct leading me more than anything else. I headed straight for the Porsche. Pulling Baby out of her parking slot, I started driving. I had no specific destination in mind. I was just drifting along behind Baby's steering wheel.

Here I was in a place that had once been home to me, but that had been too long ago. I could no longer get that feel for it. So just driving along in Baby was something like coming home. It made me feel that I was in my own territory. If I could ever drop all the tensions away and get some good, useful thinking done, it would be here.

I drove around the campus. When I passed the old buildings, memories jumped at me. There were also new dorms, new labs, other new stuff. Some of it I could identify. Much of it confused me. Resolutely I was keeping my mind off it, trying to do my thinking.

In my drifting I came within sight of the infirmary. It hit me that here there was something I had been forgetting. I was ready to say it was something we'd all been forgetting.

Sooey had not been without friends. There was Jane Struthers, and she had filled us in on much that had been going with her dead friend in the time since we had known her. But there was another friend and one who had presumably been even closer. After all, it hadn't been Jane Struthers but Alberta Smith that Sooey had chosen for her roommate. Certainly that carried the suggestion of closest friend. Sooey had confided much in Jane Struthers. Mightn't there be a good likelihood that she had confided even more in Alberta Smith? Quite aside from any such hope, it seemed obvious that, through the mere fact of their having been sharing a room, Alberta may well have been the person who had seen the most of her in her last hours.

I pulled into the infirmary parking lot, telling myself that I wasn't to expect too much. Death had come too soon. They had been roommates, but they hadn't had even one night together. There had never been that lazy interval of talk from bed to bed in the dark that may hold exchanges that just wouldn't happen in daylight. Perhaps Sooey had not been dead before bedtime, but of a certainty she had never made it back to go to bed in that room they'd been sharing.

I was also telling myself that, although talking to Alberta Smith was indeed something we'd been letting slip our minds, this couldn't be that little lost item I kept trying to remember. More and more I had the feeling that it was something small that wasn't as it should have been.

With that still haunting me, I went in and asked for Mrs. Smith. They sent me up to the infirmary roof garden. She was sitting up with a book, but she seemed happy to set it aside. I asked her how she was feeling. She said she was quite over the shock. There was a little soreness at the back of her head where she had been hit.

"But that's nothing," she said. "The basement at home has a low ceiling. I was a long time getting accustomed to it and I don't know how many times I hit my head on a ceiling beam and had just the same sort of bump. It doesn't amount to anything."

The doctors said she was all right and she was certainly feeling all right.

"In fact," she said, "it's embarrassing. I'm not at all comfortable about staying on here and soaking up all this wonderful service—nurses waiting on me and fussing over me and pampering me when I am perfectly well."

"That's what they're here for," I said.

"They're here for the sick and I'm not even the least bit sick," she said. "I was all set to leave today, but it would have meant driving home and they wanted me to have another day to settle down before I'd be taking a car on the road. I hadn't thought about that side of it, but as soon as they brought up the question of driving, I went silly and got the shakes. So I'm here till tomorrow and feeling a fraud and a fool."

"You could come back over to the Quad with us," I said, "and do your extra day of settling down among friends. You wouldn't have to do the drive home today. It's not as though you had no place else to go."

Her own words for it had been "going silly and getting the shakes." I wasn't making any such judgments, but what there was to see I was seeing. I had no more than half said it when she did come down with the shakes.

"Back to that room? No, I couldn't."

The words came in a tremulous whisper.

"I'm sure it would be no problem to get you fixed up in another room," I said.

She shook her head. Even as she was saying no, her look and the tremor of her lips were pleading with me not to frighten her even with the words.

"No," she said. "No, I couldn't."

"Okay. Forget I ever suggested it."

"I'm the world's most disgusting coward," she said. "I'm afraid of my own shadow."

"You're exaggerating. It wasn't your shadow that blipped you behind the ear."

"It wasn't just some burglar who managed to get in

there," she said. "No matter what anyone says, I know it wasn't."

"I know it, too," I said.

"You're not just saying that?"

She was all but begging me to mean what I'd said.

"Why would I just say it unless I was sure it was fact?"

"I don't know. Being kind, humoring a silly woman, trying to make her feel better about her disgusting cowardice. When Jim was alive, he was always telling me that I imagined things. I was always scaring myself with false fears. There was this horrid thing he used to quote to me. Is it 'The coward dies a thousand deaths, the brave but one'? I die the thousand deaths."

"Do you know who it was?"

"No, except that it wasn't just some burglar from outside."

"No guess? No clue?"

I was pushing.

"No," she said. "Nothing. Not that I would be saying a word if I had a glimmer or even if I knew for certain."

"Why not? Why shouldn't you say what you know?"

"I'd be too scared. I know it's shameful, but it's the way I am."

Out of all this I had been coming up with a clear sense of the way she was. That she was terrified was obvious. She was putting none of that on, and she wasn't exaggerating it. Actually for her she was being brave. I could see that she was torn. She was afraid to speak and afraid to remain silent.

The question, of course, was just what was she holding back. I could think of only two ways to read her vacillation. Either she knew her assailant or at least had a clue to his identity and was so terrified of him that she couldn't bring herself to name him, or else she knew something that gave her a clue to the reason behind the ransacking of her room. It was obviously no good pressing her. It seemed better to try to sneak up on the question.

"Of course, you don't know yet whether you've lost anything," I said.

It was a diversion and she grabbed at it. Here was something she could talk about without falling into panic.

"But I do know," she said. "People have been no end kind. They got all my things together and brought them here. I've been through everything and I know. Nothing was taken, not even so much as a pin. Everything is there unless you want to talk about my dusting powder. That was emptied out of the box. Nobody was going to sweep it up from where it was dumped all over the floor. I mean I suppose it was swept up, but nobody was going to put it back in the box and bring it to me."

"And," I said, "it wasn't as though you came in on him before he had time to find anything he wanted. He'd been through everything you had, even to the bottom of your powder box."

"That's what I've been thinking," she said.

She seemed to be sufficiently relaxed. The time had come when I could try a small push.

"It's part of what you've been thinking," I said.

"Yes," she admitted. "There is something else."

"And?"

She took several moments before she spoke again. Just watching her, I was sure I knew what she was doing with those moments. She was tucking away the words she was afraid to speak and looking for something else she could give me in their place. I was expecting that it was going to be nothing more than another of her self-accusations of cowardice, but she did much better than that.

"The way I remember it," she said, "I opened the door and I saw all that mess. That was frightening enough, but there was more. There was something that made it even more terrifying. He was still there. I knew he was still there. I don't know how I knew. Maybe I heard him breathing. Maybe it was a smell of tobacco or whiskey. I don't know. I screamed and I turned to run, but it was then that he struck me. It's not a delusion. I know that I screamed."

"You screamed," I said. "It was your screaming that brought everyone running."

"He knocked me out. That was what stopped my screaming."

I knew where she was heading, but she was edging up on it with such a high degree of timid caution that it could have taken her the better part of forever to get it said. If she ever did get there. Helping her along, I took it away from her.

"Taking it on the run," I said, "there were only two ways he could have gone. Out the entry and into the Quad would have run him smack into all the people who were jamming the entry as they rushed in to help you. He didn't take cover in any of the other rooms on the corridor. We checked those and they were empty."

"Yes," she said. "You understand what I've been thinking, but you said two ways. There isn't any other."

I was thinking that I should have said three ways, but this was no time to complicate it further. I was trying to lead her along. I didn't want to confuse her.

"You'd have to know the basement," I said. "Down

there corridors run the whole round of the dorm, entry to entry."

"Oh, then . . ."

She stopped to think about that, and she was visibly crestfallen. I was confusing her.

"But that doesn't make any difference," I said. "That's no different from going out to the Quad. The stairs to the basement are right there just inside the entry door. He couldn't have made it from your room to those basement stairs before he would have run smack into all the guys who were coming to your assistance. They would have caught him on the stairs."

"You see that then," she said.

I told her it was obvious. It was indisputable. It was solid fact. I also told her the rest of it, the conclusions that fear was holding her back from putting into words.

"That left him only the one way to go," I said. "It was down the corridor away from the stairs, away from all the guys who were rushing in."

"No," she said. "That would have taken him into a dead end."

"From which he came rushing back to mingle with the crowd of your rescuers," I said.

"Just what I've been trying not to think," Alberta said. "You were there. Maybe you can tell me something."

"I know," I said. "Of all those people who came rushing into the room, was there anyone who wasn't a member of the great and glorious class?"

She winced.

"It's a dreadful thought," she said, "but I can't make it go away."

"Facts are like that," I said. "They don't go away."

"Then?"

"Before long there were other people there. The dean, who had been in the next entry with Larry Dawson and me, some of the men who had been monitoring the Quad entrance, several of the students we have working the reunion, one kid who's been all over the place taking pictures he hopes to sell to magazines. You had screamed. All sorts of people who happened to be within hearing came rushing to you. That was inevitable. These other people, however, were later. It was a simple matter of proximity. Classmates who were out in the Quad and who happened to be closest to your entry were the first to hit the entry door and the first to come to you. The man from the gate, the kids who were working at the bars or some such and who dropped what they were doing when they heard you scream, the kid with the camera—they all had greater distances to cover. They got there later. None of them could have loitered down at the dead end of the entry corridor long enough to make as late an arrival as they did."

She shuddered.

"I just can't believe it," she said, "and yet I have to."

"Your burglar was a classmate," I said. "One of your Jim's old buddies. After all, that's the way the mythology has it, isn't it? We're all old buddies, as good as brothers."

"Of course," she said, "people do lose their minds. I suppose it can happen to anyone. They go that way and nobody notices anything till all at once it's become inescapably obvious. He's done something horrible, something irreparable."

"What he did to you was not irreparable," I said, "unless you're thinking about that box of powder."

"I was speaking in general," she said.

The hell she was. The particulars were there. She was too frightened of them to lay them before me. I took over and laid them before her. I began by telling her of the suitcase in the dean's office and the attempt that had been made on the door of the wrong room.

"What's important there is that back in the time when we were here it would have been the right room," I said. "You can see what that means? The guy wasn't interested in anything you had. He was after something Amanda Graystock had."

I had come close to calling Amanda Sooey. Pausing to give Alberta a moment to take that much in, I congratulated myself on my quickness of wit. I had pulled back from the slip even if only just in time.

"Then you don't think it's the imaginings of a silly woman who's frightened even sillier?"

"What isn't?"

I had to ask even then. I was being most careful not to put words into her mouth or an idea into her head. I wanted to be sure it was something she had come to on her own because I was going to be wanting from her every detail of what she knew, all those details that had added up to her knowledge.

"I know that Amanda didn't just die," she said. "Amanda was murdered."

"The official verdict is accidentally by her own hand," I said.

"And you don't believe it any more than I do."

"I've never believed it," I said. "But I've known stuff you didn't know, stuff that made it impossible for me to believe it."

I went on to tell her that we weren't alone in our certainty that it had been murder, and I filled her in on all the bits and pieces that had built the certainty for us—the barbiturate bottle with the label hastily scraped off, all the drinks her friend had been taking and pouring into the grass, all the fragments of evidence.

Alberta moaned.

"Then that was it," she said. "I saw the way she was carrying on all that afternoon and it worried me. I thought she was drinking far too much. It worried me partly for her. It seemed to me that she was well on the way to making a fool of herself. Selfishly it also worried me for myself. I began to be sorry that I had agreed to share the room with her. I was seeing myself having a horrible night of it with a hopelessly drunken woman on my hands."

"You didn't know that she was putting on a great act of getting plastered while all the time she was working hard at staying sober?"

"I suppose I should have known," she said. "I couldn't understand it, but I must say it never occurred to me that she was doing anything of that sort."

"You couldn't understand it? Just what couldn't you understand?"

"That last time we were alone together. We went up to the room to change for dinner. From the way I had seen her carrying on all afternoon, I expected she would be falling-down drunk. It just seemed to me that she couldn't be in any shape to go on. I was sure that when she got up to the room, she would pass out cold. I didn't think she was ever going to make dinner. I suppose I was hoping for just that. I didn't want to see her disgrace herself at the dinner table, and it seemed to me that it would have to be one or the other."

"But it wasn't," I said. "She changed for dinner and she wasn't even high."

"Oh, she was high all right," Alberta said. "She was flying. She was bubbling over with happiness. Coming to this reunion was the one smart thing she had ever done in the whole of what she was calling her stupid life. Everything was coming up roses. All her problems were solved. She was never going to have to worry again."

"Nothing more definite than that? She didn't tell you what worries she was sloughing off?"

"She didn't have to go into that. I knew her problem."

She went on to give me what I'd already had from Jane Struthers. The worries had been financial, although Jane had had it that Sooey had been inordinately blithe about her situation. Now I was gathering that she had revealed more of her true feelings to Alberta than she had to Jane. That carefree, something-always-turns-up attitude had been a front. Behind it she had been frightened of the future and not of a temperament to do anything prudent about it.

"You see," Alberta said, "money worries were something she had never had before. For her it was something completely new and she didn't have even the first idea of how she might cope."

In explaining that to me, she told me much that I had never known about Sooey. I could now remember that in my undergraduate days when I had known her she had never wanted for funds. At the time it hadn't occurred to me to think about it. Back then it wasn't anything that any of us thought about. Money was what your old man shelled out to cover the bills you bucked on to him, and otherwise it was the allowance check you were expected to stretch over the whole month.

Times when you overestimated its elasticity and came up short, you wrote a letter or made a phone call to touch up the old man for what you called an advance on next month's allowance. Of course you knew and he knew that you were asking for something extra. That brought you the obligatory sermon on learning the value of a buck and the reminder that they didn't grow on trees.

I grant you, there were the guys who were working their way through college and I wasn't so insulated that none of these were among my friends, but I ran with the beef-and-brawn bunch. They had their scholarships and their student loans. They had unexacting campus jobs that paid disproportionately well, and summers there was always one alumnus or another who backed the team by providing summer jobs that demanded little and paid a lot. Even those guys were pretty well protected from learning much about how men out in the real world earned their bucks.

So back in those days when I hadn't been giving it a thought, Sooey had been an orphan alone in the world, but in no way exposed to its rigors. There had been trust funds and lawyers and bank to administer them. So she had been like us. Money had been something that came in at regular intervals and there had been more of it than she ever needed.

At the time when we had made the big change of going out on our own and we learned, since the pockets were now our own, that even the deepest pockets had bottoms, for Sooey nothing changed. There did come the time when she had reached the age at which her forebears had expected she would have become mature enough to take on the management of her own financial affairs. At that time the trusts had been dissolved and she had come into the principal of the trust funds.

"Poor Amanda was never the flitter-witted fool she pretended to be," Alberta said. "She never deluded herself that she could be competent to do anything about money other than spend it, and she wasn't about to try. The lawyers and the bank had been managing very well for her. In their hands her money grew and her income kept increasing. She wasn't one of those idiots who can't wait till they will be permitted to mess around with their investments."

Well satisfied with what her trustees had been doing for her, Sooey had simply perpetuated the arrangement, hiring them for the management of her affairs.

"So how come the financial bind?" I asked. "What went sour?"

"George Graystock," Alberta said.

She knew the whole story and in detail. Back in the old days we had known him as God-Damn Gruesome; what she was now telling me had me amending it to God-Damn Greedy. He had gone through life convinced all the way that he was a financial genius. That most of what he touched went sour and none of the rest of it was ever very great hadn't disturbed his illusions. It was never lack of judgment that had been at fault, it was always the lack of a stake large enough to match his imagination. All he needed was the money to work with and he'd be bringing off the great coups.

"So that was it," Alberta said. "When they married, Amanda took everything she had out of the hands of the very competent people she'd had handling it for her and she gave George that adequate stake he'd always wanted."

"With which he demonstrated that he could be as incompetent with large sums as he had been with small," I said.

"I thought so," Alberta said, "but now I'm wondering if perhaps it wasn't entirely his own fault."

She came up with a theory. Wasn't it possible that he'd had some big deal with an old buddy in the class and old buddy had taken him to the cleaners, even to the extent of something like embezzlement?

"Suppose Amanda came on the evidence of it," she said. "She brought it here to reunion and confronted the crook with what she knew and told him she had hard evidence of it. Could she have been so high because she thought she had pushed him into making restitution? So they had a drink together on it, and that was it."

It was something to think about. We had been so obsessed with Sooey's amatory history that it hadn't occurred to us to think in any other terms. As soon as I began thinking about it, I began going off it.

"I don't know," I said. "As I remember Graystock, I can't think that, when it came to ruining himself, he would need assistance. I can picture him doing it on nothing more than his own stupidity."

"Yes," Alberta said. "But then I never liked him. I shouldn't be saying this, I suppose, but I always thought he married her for the money."

"Except that he didn't marry her," I said.

"You know that then? Yes, it's true. They lived together without ever marrying, but I'd put it that she never married him. He was determined that they should marry and she was determined that they wouldn't. They had a great struggle over it, but as soon as he found that he had complete control over her money anyhow, he calmed down. I think that's why she was so ready to give him complete control, even in the face of everyone's advice to the contrary. She was leaning over backward to make him feel that she was at least as much his—even abjectly his—as she could have been if they had made it official. She had this feeling that she had to compensate him for the fact that she couldn't marry him."

There was the one word and I picked up on it. Up to that time, as she had been telling it and as Jane Struthers had told it, it had been a matter of *wouldn't*. *Couldn't* was another animal.

"You said 'couldn't'?"

"Her word," Alberta said. "It's what she told me—in complete confidence, of course. Her insistence on not marrying was not a whim and it wasn't a matter of principle or anything like that. It was simply that she couldn't marry anyone."

"Just couldn't? No reason why?"

"She couldn't tell me the reason. She couldn't tell anyone."

CHAPTER 7

So now I had something that called for heavy thought. This was Sooey Generous that we were talking about—good old fun-in-bed, happy-go-lucky, uncomplicated Sooey. Suddenly I was asked to think about her as though she were a character out of Ibsen. It was easier to conceive of Martha Washington as Marcel Proust might have written her. I said as much to Alberta.

"Exactly," she said. "I've never been able to understand it or to equate it with Amanda as I knew her, and I've had a long time to think about it, ever since they were first married." Catching herself, she rushed into a correction. "I know, I know," she said. "But how can you put it? 'Ever since they were first not married'? You know, it was simply impossible to think of them that way. The way they were with each other, the way they lived—it was Victorian, pure Darby and Joan."

An old adage went racing through my mind: "There's no one so righteous as a reformed whore."

I didn't say it, and I discarded it as quickly as I'd thought of it. It was glib, but I couldn't make it fit. I was guessing that it was more like her old-fashioned wifely stupidity about giving him the management of her money. She was refusing to marry the guy but she was doing everything heaped up and running over to demonstrate to him that she was no less abjectly his than she might have been if they had gone through the full bell-book-and-candle routine.

I put all that away for thinking about later. I went over another aspect of what Alberta Smith had been telling me, one on which I could hope she might have some answers.

"The smartest thing she'd ever done was coming to reunion," I said. "Everything was coming up roses. All her problems were solved. Was it just that? No specifics? No hints? Pot of gold at the end of the beer bar? What?"

"She didn't say and I didn't ask."

"No curiosity? I would have been curious."

"I thought I knew, and I couldn't see where it could be anything as good as she was imagining, but she was so happy over it that I didn't want to go rushing in to throw the cold water."

"What did you think it was?"

Her friend Amanda had been saying for some time that sooner or later the money would be running out and she was going to have to find herself a job. As time had passed, she had come around to thinking it would better be sooner than later, that she shouldn't wait until she was flat broke.

"She came here, it seemed to me, with the idea that one or another of you men would find her a job. She had come to realize that, if she was going to get a job, it couldn't be on her qualifications. It would have to be on her contacts. So it seemed obvious to me that what she was doing all that afternoon was working on her contacts."

"She worked on me and on the guys I was drinking with at the time she came over," I said. "She said nothing about job hunting, not a word about problems."

Alberta nodded.

"I didn't know that but, even if I had known it, I would have thought that she had looked over the ground and that

she had her selected targets, men who control so many jobs
that they could find a place to fit her in. You know, something like receptionist in some executive's outer office.
Nothing to it but announcing people and making them
feel comfortable while they are kept waiting. She could
have done something like that."

"So you just assumed she had landed a thing of that sort
and she was building it into something a lot bigger than it
possibly could be. You thought she was building herself up
to the roughest kind of letdown and you were in no hurry
to tell her as much."

"It was more than that," Alberta said. "She was thinking
that she had come up with something very special, something far better than anything she had dreamed of. That
was how it seemed to me, and I thought I knew what it
was and I didn't trust it."

"You no longer think so?"

"I can't see it as anything that could ever possibly have
gotten her murdered."

"Let me have a look at it."

"Have you met Mrs. Roberts—Mrs. Hamilton Roberts?"

"Call me Glad," I said.

"You've met her. I'm going to sound like a cat."

"Don't give it a thought. Just go on and sound."

"I suppose Glad Roberts wouldn't have talked to you
about her problems. It was sort of girl talk."

"What to do about a husband who hands her an eyeful
of fist?" I asked.

"No. She never said anything about that, not to me at
least. It was her problems with shopping."

"Oh, come on!"

I couldn't make anything of that unless it was the onset
of nonsense. I wanted Alberta back on the ball. I was

wrong. She wasn't wandering. With Glad Roberts girl talk had been about nothing but shopping. Glad had filled the other girls in on her peculiar and grievous plight. In the places where she and Ham lived there was nothing to buy. It was all right for jewelry, but for clothes and accessories it was hopeless.

"She kept talking about how other women could get to Paris and Rome and Milan every season for the showings and for their fittings," Alberta said, "but she could never make it. It was always that her husband couldn't get away at the right times and she couldn't go off and leave him." She stopped in some confusion. I put in the few nudging words. "I don't like talking about another woman this way and I probably shouldn't be doing it, but then you might see something in it that I've been missing."

"Yes," I said. "For instance, did she say anything about why she couldn't go off and leave him even for such urgent necessities as dress fittings?"

Alberta worked hard at doing it deadpan.

"Their great love," she said. "Undying passion and not only undying but unremitting as well. They have never been apart for even one night since the day they were married. Ham would be lost without his Glad. She could never do that to the poor boy."

"And you don't believe a word of it."

She studied me for a moment.

"You never married," she said.

"Never."

"Then maybe I should tell you. Marriage isn't like that. I had a good marriage with Jim Smith, even a great marriage. We missed each other when we were apart and I shall never get over missing him now that he's gone, but there's no togetherness that is not the better for being sweetened by periodic spells of apartness. People who are not successful alone can never form a successful couple."

"And you have ideas about why she can never leave him?" I asked.

"If he were ill, seriously ill, but it's obviously not that."

"So?"

"With or without reason he's so jealous that he will never let her out of his sight," Alberta said.

"Or," I said, "with or without reason she's so jealous that she'll go naked in jewelry before she'll ever let him out of her sight."

"One or the other, and I'm inclined toward yours."

We swapped impressions and she filled me in on all the gossip.

"I'm telling you this," she said, "only because I was almost certain that Amanda's great joy was over having landed what she thought was going to be a dream job. Gladys Roberts had been going on and on about how she had to find someone who could be a shopping agent for her. She needed a woman of taste who could be relied on to know what would suit Gladys. The woman would have to have the same measurements as Gladys so she could stand in for her in the fittings. Her idea was that she would pay such a woman well. The woman would go to all the couturier showings in Paris and Rome and Milan and so on."

With her woman's eye for such things, Alberta had observed that Glad Roberts and her poor, ingenuous friend Sooey were the same size, the same shape, and in every respect the same body type. She told me that it was obvious that the two women could wear each other's clothes. It seemed to her that this was what Sooey was taking to be her great windfall.

"All that European travel with all expenses paid, unlimited funds for buying, good pay, and a lavish expense account," she said. "You could hardly call it work. Any woman would have great fun doing it. Also anyone buying on that scale would have the designers competing for her custom. She would be in line for great gifts. Nobody would call them bribes, of course, but they would be there."

"But still you thought she was deluding herself. Why?"

"You're going to think I'm the world's worst cat," she said.

"No. An intelligent woman of great common sense."

"All right. I just couldn't believe it would be there. Glad Roberts, I would say, is a woman best taken with more than a grain of salt. I thought all her talk came to no more than an elaborately contrived form of boasting. At best I thought it might be her daydream and that, when it actually came down to it, the whole thing would just evaporate. My only other thought about it was that working for Gladys Roberts would be pure hell. If Amanda had ever so much as gotten started on it, it couldn't have lasted long, and every minute of it would have been a disaster. I suppose what it really comes down to is that I very much dislike the Roberts woman."

"That's understandable," I said, "but, as it turned out, you had the whole thing all wrong. Amanda must have been following some other line of work."

"It does seem so," she said, "but there is one other thing and it has me wondering."

"What other thing?"

"The Roberts woman's so-called accident."

"The black eye?"

"You know the Hoyts? Florence Hoyt was in their room with the Roberts pair in the room next door. She heard them quarreling, and from the sound of it she hadn't the first doubt. She was certain that he was beating her. She said it was horrible listening to it and not being able to do anything about it. Her husband wasn't there and without him she thought she couldn't do anything. Of course that was silly of her. She could so easily have found some of you men, or she could have gone next door herself. In her place I would have done just that."

"You see a connection?"

"Florence Hoyt heard them screaming at each other. They were quarreling about Amanda. She couldn't hear all of it, so she didn't know just *what* about Amanda, but she did know that much. He was saying horrible things about Amanda and raging at his wife about her having anything to do with a woman of Amanda's sort. Those words Florence did hear clearly—'a woman of Amanda's sort.' I can't imagine what he would have meant by that, unless somehow he knew about her and Graystock not having been married, because in every way Amanda was a much nicer woman than that incredible wife of his."

"They make a good pair," I said.

"Is it possible . . . ?" she began.

"That it was so important to him that he keep his wife and 'a woman of that sort' apart that he beat up on Glad and then, to make absolutely sure they'd never get together, he murdered Amanda? No. There has to be more to it than that. Why search your room? Why the attempt to get at Amanda's suitcase? What does he think she had that he must get his hands on? She had something the killer needed to get away from her, or at least she led him to believe she had it. It was something he felt was worth killing for, and now he needs it more desperately than ever.

Whatever it was he feared from it before, now it's something that might convict him of murder."

"They're so filthy rich," Alberta said.

"They appear to be."

"Jim used to say that under laws as they are and have been in our time, it's next to impossible for a man to get very rich staying inside the law."

She was reaching for something but it seemed like a fumbling reach.

"You're thinking that maybe Ham got his by embezzling Amanda's money away from Graystock," I said. "You think she had that much?"

"If that's the way he made his money, then he could have taken other people, too. His wife was talking all that nonsense about the shopping. Can't it be that Amanda saw herself as perfect for the job? She would have been, if there ever had been such a job. Couldn't Amanda have been thinking she could have it? She would confront him with what she knew about him. She would tell him that he owed her. He would make Gladys take her on. Something like that."

I found myself wanting to believe it. I had to tell myself that it was only my dislike of Ham Roberts that was making it seem credible.

"He's not looking for anything very big," I said. "It's something so small that it could be hidden in a box of dusting powder. Proof of embezzlement, I should think, would have to be more than that, a whole filing cabinet full of papers. Let's remember that he emptied your powder box."

"You know," she said, "I suppose it's because I'm frightened, but I'm not at all convinced that, when he ransacked my things, he did it with any mistaken idea that they were Amanda's."

"When he learned that her bag had been taken out of the room and was locked away in the dean's office, he did try to get at it there."

"Yes. I understand that, but it doesn't say that he didn't think that he had to search both my things and hers."

"Why?" I asked.

"I think I'm safe here," she said, "although even here I'm nervous. But there are the two of us who were her close friends, Jane Struthers and myself. I worry about Jane. Suppose he's thinking that the thing he's after Amanda might have given to Jane or me to hold for her. That's what I mean about his searching my things and Amanda's. I'm afraid for Jane. I keep thinking he might go after her, too."

"I hardly think that," I said. "Not now. He would have done it before this."

She shook her head.

"No," she said. "Now more than ever. Once he learns that Amanda's bag has been searched and there was nothing in it, isn't he going to begin thinking about other places it might be, other people who might have it? Her friends?"

"How's he going to learn that?"

"There were many witnesses, weren't there?" she said. "When that many people are in on something—the more people the greater the chance of a leak."

I made all the reassuring noises I could think of, but only because there was nothing to be gained from confirming her in her terrors. Privately I couldn't get far with discounting them. I had a picture of the police chief and the mayor spreading the story of how the band of amateur Sherlocks had demanded a search of the dead woman's suitcase only to fall on their silly faces.

Hauling back to the Quad I was not without more than enough to think about, but it added up to too many questions and not even one reasonable answer. I had no sooner hit the Quad than I was engulfed by my fellow detectives. Where had I been? What had I been doing? I had given them the fright of their lives.

"Fright?" I asked. "What's to be afraid of?"

"We must all stick together every minute of the time," Slammer said, speaking for the lot of them. "Nobody goes off on his own."

"A great idea," I said, "since we're all such good company, but again what's to be afraid of?"

They were patient with me. They explained it to me. They were even trying to hold it down to words of one syllable. We were the ones who were crying murder, and we were the only ones. Did I expect the killer to take kindly to that? So it was to be safety in numbers and all that crap.

They were having pictures of big, bad classmate just waiting for a chance to cut one of us away from the pack so he could pick us off one by one. I don't think either Larry or Bob had fallen into any such state of timorousness. It was more likely that they were afraid of being dealt out on any action that might come up. Slammer and Jane Struthers, however, constantly looking back over their shoulders, had gone dizzy from all that head turning. The guys, even if for their own reasons, were indulging them.

We had to get past all that nonsense before they came around to giving me a message they had for me. My young friend Tommy had been looking for me. When I went looking for Tommy, therefore, the whole gang trailed

along. It was okay. After all, I was having no secrets from
them.

It was a bad time for pulling the kid away from his
duties. The afternoon program had finished. People were
flocking back to the Quad and bringing their accumulated
thirsts with them. The bars were three deep and the kids
doing the bartending were taking orders with both ears and
pouring with both hands.

Tommy couldn't take time out for more than a few
words and even then only while he was doing the pouring
for me and my entourage.

"I think I maybe have a line on your creep," he said.
"But with all these tongues hanging out, I can't break
away till we've got most of them tucked back in. Where
will you be?"

Larry and Bob were in the process of snagging a table
and settling the girls at it. Even while they were doing that,
they weren't for a moment taking their eyes off me. Obviously they were expecting me to join them. I indicated the
table.

"Right there," I said. "Whenever you can make it."

Meanwhile the party at the table was growing. Florence
Hoyt was joining the others, bringing her drink over and
sitting down with them. Ever since the Hoyt-Roberts bout
this had become something of a pattern.

Every time Culver went off somewhere and left his
Florence on her own even for a moment, she immediately
went looking for Slammer. She had come to think of Slammer, if not of the rest of our little group, as her best in-
sulation against the embarrassment of an encounter with
Ham Roberts or his Glad. By the time I'd broken away
from Tommy at the bar, Culver had also turned up. I let

myself hope that he would take his Florence away, but he didn't. He pulled up a chair and joined the party.

"What did the enormous child want with you?" Slammer asked. "When he came looking for you, he made it sound urgent."

I explained about what I had asked of the boy. "He thinks he has line on who the peeper was," I said.

"Any good?" Larry asked.

Everyone was interested, but for Larry there was a special eagerness to his interest just as there was for me. It had, after all, been the pair of us who had messed up that encounter. We were feeling the responsibility.

"He'll be over to explore it with us as soon as he can break away," I said.

So it was just to wait and kick it around while we were waiting. There wouldn't have been much to kick around if it hadn't been for the Hoyts. An undergraduate Peeping Tom of the shaggy persuasion was boringly up their alley. We got the whole package. Culver had known it all along. In our day we hadn't had any murderers. The university admissions office of our day had protected us from all that. Only gentlemen had been admitted then, boys who had been brought up in the great traditions of the great old place.

"What about Larry and Matt and me?" Bob asked.

"What about you?" Culver said. "You came from good families. You came from good prep schools. You and Matt were alumni sons."

"Okay," Larry said. "My old man went to Harvard. You don't have to rub it in. He was a reformed character. Didn't he atone by letting me come here?"

We tried to kid him out of it. Various efforts were made to change the subject, but Culver Hoyt had mounted his favorite hobby horse and he was riding it hard. He also had his lady up behind him and nothing could persuade either of them to dismount.

It was only when Tommy had come over to join us that they shut up. They did a great deal more than shut up. They froze. It took only the sight of his name plate. His morass of Ss, Cs, Ws, and Zs identified him as part of the "class" they had been belaboring. I wished that he might have been a Latin or a black. That would have done more than freeze them, it would have reminded them that they had a most pressing engagement elsewhere. As it was, we weren't quite rid of them. They stayed put in disapproving silence, obviously expecting a demonstration of what they had been pushing at us.

"One question," Tommy said. "Your creep—just when was it that you saw him?"

"The first night, Wednesday," I said.

Larry pinned it down more precisely. "It was just before we came on Mrs. Graystock's body," he said.

Tommy broke out in a happy grin.

"All I needed to know," he said. "I've got him for you."

"Here that night but took off right afterwards?" I asked.

"Oh, no. He's still around. If you ask me, he's too much around; but it's not for me to say, not as long as your reunion committee is all eager to hold still for him."

"Around here in the Quad?" Larry asked.

"We haven't been seeing him," I said, "and we have been looking."

"You wouldn't know him," Tommy said. "I hardly knew him myself. His name's Dowling—Rick Dowling."

It was a bad letdown. I could think of nothing to say. I was thinking that I had overestimated Tommy in assuming he had a brain to go with his muscles. However insufficient my description, it had been more than enough to rule out the ubiquitous young cameraman.

Larry spoke for both of us. "The paparazzo," he said. "Impossible."

"Pappa who?" Tommy asked.

"The obnoxious lad with the camera," Larry said.

"That's our man, Rick."

"We know that one," I said. "He's nothing like this other guy. Dowling is so preppy you can hardly believe him."

Tommy laughed.

"The preppiest ever," he said. "You shouldn't believe him. That morning when I first saw him, I couldn't. Haircut that's got him only one short jump short of being a skinhead, shave, and from the chin on down all pure Brooks Brothers. It's so very much too much, you could think maybe he's kidding it."

Culver Hoyt glowered, but Florence Hoyt was just not taking any of this from someone she had already identified as a young guttersnipe. She spoke up.

"He's clean and neat," she said. "He's properly dressed and well-mannered. Would you, please, tell me what's so hilarious about that?"

"Yes, ma'am," Tommy said. "What's so funny about it is that he isn't. He isn't any of those things. Clean? All year he's maybe never showered even once. Neat? The only combing his hair or his beard ever got was with his fingers when he was scratching, and he was scratching all the time. Properly dressed? Alongside him you would have thought I was Beau Brummel, which you can see I'm not. What does that leave? Well-mannered? I wouldn't know about well-mannered. That could be, but only for a pig."

I listened to all of that and so did Larry. Like me, of

course, he was busily straightening things around inside his head.

"You mean right after we saw him, just overnight," I asked, "the total clean up—haircut, shave, sudden acquisition of the preppiest of preppy wardrobes?"

"Disguise," Larry said, "and it worked. At least up to now it worked."

"We caught him at the keyhole," I said. "There wouldn't be a chance that he wouldn't be questioned and for whatever reason he doesn't want to be questioned. So he fixed it. We couldn't have spotted him or identified him in a million years."

Tommy looked dubious.

"Maybe not," he said. "More likely he's just going home for the summer. I can see it. He goes home the way he always is around here. His old man catches him on his way in the door and throws him right back out. It would be the never-darken-my-door-again routine."

I was still finding it incredible. I was even fantasizing about the possibility of getting Rick Dowling with his pants off. There would be positive marks of identification where Larry and I had landed our kicks.

Tommy took care of my doubts. He explained Rick Dowling to us. That his explanation might have been targeted directly for the Culver Hoyts may possibly have been an accident. It is my guess, though, that Tommy knew precisely where he was hitting home and that his every word was chosen to be precisely on target. Culver, after all, had been sounding off all over the place with his opinions of the modern undergraduate, and Florence had been echoing him with the addition of embellishments that were all her own.

"I know more about Rick Dowling than most of the

guys," Tommy said, "because my old man is in steel and so is his. There's a difference, of course. His old man is chairman of the board, and when steel business isn't as good as Paul Dowling likes it's my old man that gets laid off for a while."

"That Dowling?" Culver said. "Paul Dowling's son?"

He spoke the name with reverence. In the university context it seemed as though there had always been Dowlings. Live Dowlings were heavy contributors. Dead Dowlings were commemorated in Dowling Hall, the Dowling dorm complex, and the Dowling Tower. In a broader context Dowlings were friends of presidents, it was generally recognized that Dowlings had senators and congressmen in their pockets, and foreign policy was never unaware of Dowling affection for questionable kings and dictators.

"Just to look at him," Florence said, "I knew that he came of good family."

"Just to look at him now, ma'am," Tommy said. "If you had seen him before he pulled up his socks to go home, you'd have thought he was scum. I hear that what this place needs is more like him. I don't know. Maybe. Maybe he's good for funding. No telling how much his daddy's been kicking in to keep Rick from being kicked out."

"There's something here I don't understand," Slammer said. "No Dowling can possibly be wanting for money. The boy is all over the place with his camera. He drools visibly in anticipation of the money he'll be paid for his pictures."

"He has expensive habits," Tommy said. "I wouldn't know, but I guess they're so expensive that he can't finance them out of the money from home, even though the money from home has got to be plenty good and even though he goes all year saving on soap and haircuts."

Culver took exception.

"That's nonsense," he said. "When people like the Dowlings don't bring their sons up to know the value of a dollar, when they don't encourage them to show enterprise and go out and earn money on their own, they breed kids who'll never be anything but wastrels and playboys. The lad should be praised for his industry."

"I suppose so," Tommy said. "Me? I learned the value of a buck through never having many of them. I don't know how the rich can go about it unless it's by finding ways of not having enough. Rick smokes only the best grass. Also it's been said around that cocaine has become the drug of the affluent upper classes. In that department Rick is upper class, nobody more upper."

I don't know whether he was more bent on convincing us that we had our man or on enjoying the all-too-manifest fact that everything he was saying was one in the eye for the Hoyts. Whichever, he did have the lot of us convinced. Maybe I had better particularize that. The lot of us didn't include Florence and Culver.

Tommy returned to his duties and the Hoyts spoke their minds.

"There is nothing more disgusting than envy," Florence said. "I must say I have never witnessed such a horrid exhibition."

I had vivid memories of the way she looked at the Roberts diamonds and emeralds. It was not unlikely that she was something of an authority on envy.

"It's more than envy," Culver said. "If you check him out, I'll bet you'll find that his father is one of those reds, a union agitator."

"I don't believe a word of that nonsense about drugs,"

Florence said. "Anyone can see with half an eye that he isn't the type."

Larry picked her up on that.

"I've looked at a lot of them with a whole eye," he said. "Addicts who have the money to support their habit go around looking very much like you and me. It's the poor who show it, and most of what they show comes from malnutrition and from despair and panic. They live in perpetual anxiety, never knowing whether they are going to be able to manage the next fix or how."

"All the same," Florence said, "he's the only student we've seen around here who knows how to behave properly."

"You didn't see him in his other manifestation," I said, "before he cleaned himself up. Larry and I did."

"We," Larry said, "might even take credit for his proper behavior. We gave him a lesson in it."

"If you believe it's the same boy," Culver said.

Obviously neither Hoyt was disposed to believe anything of the sort.

"Matt's young friend," Larry said, "is wrong about only one thing. I don't know how much the Dowling brat would have felt he had to shape up before going home for the summer, but I can't believe he would have gone to such extremes. Even the best families have learned to accept longer hair than that crew cut. This preppy deal isn't for the chairman of the board. It's for Matt and me. It's disguise."

"It's only the way boys of his class are supposed to look," Culver contributed.

"Supposed by whom?" Bob asked.

"By people who have chosen not to abandon all standards," Culver said.

Slammer came up out of her chair.

"I'm for joining the lower classes," she said. "The air up here is getting too thin to breathe."

CHAPTER 8

It was with a certain degree of coolness, therefore, that we broke away from the upper-class Hoyts. We retired to the Careys' room for a council of war. The company was of two minds and the split was along the line of gender. Slammer and Jane were advocating our taking no action except through official channels.

"You do nothing but tell the dean," Slammer said.

I was in anything but a do-nothing mood and I could sense that Larry and Bob were having feelings neatly matched to mine. I came up with a nifty reason for keeping the whole thing away from Dean Danny Mulligan until after we'd had our own session with Rick Dowling and we had everything pinned down to hand it to Dean Danny complete and gift-wrapped.

"The creep isn't just any creep," I said. "He's a Dowling, one of those Dowlings. There's no point in embarrassing the dean by pushing him into making the first move. Hand him the *fait accompli* and then he can take all necessary action without creating problems for the university. He'll be in a position to plead no choice."

"You have a point," Jane Struthers said, "but it doesn't matter."

"It matters," Bob told her. "Take it from me, speaking from academia, trustees don't take kindly to faculty, even at the dean level, if it shows any disposition to kill the creep that lays the golden eggs."

"I understand that," Jane said. "I said it doesn't matter because this isn't a thing for the university. Murder isn't some bit of nonsense that can be handled in the dean's office with a reprimand or probation or suspension or even expulsion. You should stop thinking like alumni and begin thinking like citizens. Murder is a crime against the state."

"Right enough," Bob said, "but we've come to know that police chief. He's over his head in this. He's so far out of his depth that he doesn't need this thrown at him. He needs a life belt."

"And," Larry said, "if the university is going to be in something of a bind because of the Dowling largesse, you might expect the university to grit its institutional teeth and do the right thing. You can't expect anything from the police chief. Police chiefs are small-time politicians, and even big-time politicians lie down and roll over in the presence of money, even when it's not nearly of the size of the Dowling money."

"We get the truth out of young Rick," I said, "and we take it to Dean Danny. That way, if he likes, he can even pretend that Rick was a hero and volunteered it. The dean will take the news to the police chief. It'll be everything through channels with Larry and me as the first channel."

Bob wasn't holding still for that.

"What counts me out?" he asked.

"You didn't kick him in the ass," Larry said.

"Which makes it my turn," Bob said. "So all the more reason it will be the three of us."

Slammer turned to Jane.

"Do we let the male chauvinist pigs ease us out?" she asked.

"If they're going to be violent with the boy," Jane said, "I'd just as soon be eased out."

"The very reason we have to be there," Slammer said. "To keep them in order."

Larry turned to Bob.

"How come Hobie Struthers got his wife trained properly and you haven't?" he asked.

"Hobie didn't marry a female chauvinist sow," Bob said.

Slammer laughed. "And proud of it," she said.

We'd had the door shut on this discussion, but now we were interrupted by a polite knock. For a moment I let myself hope that it might be the young lens man come to take more pictures. Before anyone said 'Come in,' however, I'd already decided that it wouldn't be. He had already tested out his disguise on us. He wasn't likely to go on pushing it. He had also run afoul of us when we were taking Alberta Smith through the Quad on her way to her infirmary refuge. It seemed to me that ever since, although we had been seeing him around with his incessant shutter-clicking, he had been giving us a wide berth.

Now that I was thinking about it, it came to me that I couldn't remember exactly when it had been that I had last seen him. He had been nowhere in evidence while we had been waiting for Tommy to come and talk to us, and he hadn't been around during the time when Tommy had been telling us about him.

I had the uncomfortable thought that he had caught all the pictures he might have had any hope of selling and had pulled out, skipped town. I also began wondering whether Tommy had come around to thinking of him all on his own or if possibly there had been something of an encounter between the two of them. Had Tommy, one way or another, given him a warning that we would soon be catching

up with him or had Tommy made some move against him
on his own? I could well imagine the Dowling boy scut-
tling away from that. There couldn't be too many people
who wouldn't.

At least to the extent that it wasn't Rick Dowling at the
door, my guesses were good. It was Glad and Ham Roberts, now, as a result of the room swap, next-door neighbors
to the Careys.

"Hi, kids," Ham said. "Can we come in?"

"You are in," Bob said.

It wasn't the most gracious welcome, but Ham laughed.

"So we are," he said. "So we are."

"Anything on your mind?" I asked.

I was thinking of all that stuff I'd had from Alberta and
I was trying to fit the silly lug into the role of murderer. I
was running it through the routine of the wife-beater who
misjudges his strength when he's beating up on a woman
and as a result she comes up dead. I could almost make it
look good except for the one thing. Sooey hadn't been
beaten to death.

Hers had been the skillful and gentle murder. Neither
skillful nor gentle would be what I was ready to call Ham's
style. Okay, not for ham-handed Ham, but for which of
the great old gang?

"On my mind?" Ham said. "Nothing on my mind.
There's nothing up there but hair, and not as much of that
as there used to be."

Slammer was doing the hostess turn. She had Bob busy
making them drinks. As Glad took hers, she was setting the
condition that sometime before we'd all be pulling out we
were to come to them next door.

"We have champagne," she said. "You like champagne?"

"Preferable to the real thing," Larry said.

"It's Dom Perignon. The real thing? What's that?"

He had her worried. Could there be something more snob than champagne that she didn't know about?

"Real pain."

It came in unison from Bob, Larry, Slammer, and me. It was a gag out of the old days and evidently Bob had trained Slammer up in it. Glad just looked bewildered till she noticed that Jane was laughing.

"Oh," she said then. "Oh, yes. A joke."

"Of sorts," Slammer said. "Only of sorts. Not screamingly funny, but the guys have a sentimental attachment to it."

That was no help. It just confused Glad the more. Ham changed the subject.

"Before we came over from next door," he asked, "did I hear somebody say Dowling?"

"It's a name that's heard around here," I said.

"Dowling Hall, Dowling Dorms," Larry added.

"It gets to have a familiar ring," Bob said.

"That's a great man, Paul Dowling," Ham said. "He's maybe the greatest ever went here."

"We've had Nobel Prize winners and we've had guys who grew up to be president of the United States, if you call that growing up," Bob said.

"Maybe them," Ham conceded, "but they weren't in our time."

"Was Paul Dowling?" Slammer asked.

"Our freshman year," Ham said, "Paul was a junior."

His tone indicated that this would be something that added mightily to our stature. Slammer turned to Bob.

"And you never told me."

Her awestruck act was perfect.

"Nobody told me he was going to be so rich," Bob said. "I just took no notice of him."

"He was the only man on campus who had his private jet," Ham said. "He flew everywhere."

Bob beamed at him.

"Then that's it," he said. "I rarely raised my eyes above hemlines, so naturally I was unaware of anything way up there."

"Did you know his son is on campus?" Ham asked. "Actually he lives right here in the dorm just like anybody else. I like that. That's democracy."

"More democratic," Slammer said, "than having his own jet and spending all his time up above everyone else."

"He's the nice looking kid who's been taking all the pictures," Ham persisted. "The minute I first saw him, it struck me. He looked familiar, and, of course, he's the spitting image of his dad, just like Paul when he was in college. He's a real chip off the old block."

"And he knows the value of a buck," Larry said.

"How not? It's in the blood," Ham said. "He's a Dowling. Have you gotten a good look at his cameras? Beautiful."

"We've been seeing him around but not just recently," I said. "Have you seen him? Let's say this afternoon?"

"Out in the Quad he's around all the time," Ham said. "You want to see cameras what are cameras, you just watch for him out there."

"We sure do want to see cameras what are cameras," Bob said.

I said nothing, but I just couldn't believe that was going to do it. It may well have been no more than impatience to get my hands on the young bastard. I don't like to make a claim to having any sixth sense—there are times when I'm not sure it isn't boasting for me to say I have even all of the standard five.

So let's leave it that I had a hunch. Young Dowling was not going to be all that easy to find. My hunch was telling me that it wasn't even that he had pulled out for his summer at home. For one reason or another I was thinking that the kid had gone to earth. Somebody was going to have to find his hidey-hole and root him out of it.

It had come to dinner time and I told myself that would be the test. I suddenly remembered when I had last seen the boy. It had been at lunch. He had been there with his camera. He had, in fact, not missed any meal we'd had at any time since his transformation.

It didn't seem possible that he had any notion that there would be an enormous market for shots taken of us when we were feeding. I had to think that the Hoyt-Roberts fracas had whetted his appetite and that mealtimes ever since had kept him on hand and alert for another such spectacular. Thinking back, I came down with the realization that on his mealtime appearances he had been hovering steadfastly within camera range of either Culver or Ham.

I could only think that he had been hoping for another encounter between those two. I was even trying to tell myself that I was thinking with his mind. That was getting to be a habit, thinking with other people's minds. Maybe because I wasn't too enamored of the thinking that had been coming out of my own mind. If he had noticed that Culver and Ham were at all times keeping maximum distance between them, he could easily have been going along on the hope that, if they were to come into proximity at all, it was going to be at a meal. After all, it was only then that they were brought together in the same room.

I watched for Rick Dowling all through dinner, but he never showed. I tried to catch Tommy's attention, but he was one busy behemoth. Short of my taking a swing at one of the old buddies and setting up a situation where he would have to abandon more routine duties for his emergency role of peacemaker, I hadn't a chance until the last cup of after-dinner coffee had been served.

I held my impatience in check. When the time came that he could break loose, I didn't have to go after him. He came to me. He had been catching my signals.

"I thought he'd be around at dinner," I said, "but he hasn't shown. When did you see him last?"

"Not since lunch," Tommy said. "He was here taking pictures at lunch."

"Did you say anything to him?" I asked. "Maybe giving him a hint that would have made him take off away from here?"

"The morning he first turned up with the camera, I gave him a lot more than a hint, but he went over my head to your reunion committee and they didn't back me up on it. So that shut my big, fat mouth. I haven't had anything to say to him since."

"Then something else gave him the idea it was time to move out," I said. "I'm wondering what and who."

"Look," Tommy said. "By now he's taken more pictures than he'll ever sell anywhere. It's no sure thing that he's taken off. Could be he's only run out of film."

"Does he room here in the dorm, or did he make some special arrangement with the reunion committee that let him come in and out of the Quad?"

"No special arrangement. He lives here. Lucky me, he's on my entry."

Tommy gave me the room number. It was going to be

no problem finding the room. I knew exactly where it was, directly across the hall from a room where we'd been spending a lot of reunion time, the room where, ever since they'd swapped with the Hoyts, Slammer and Bob had been hosting our councils of war.

"I'll try the room," I said.

"If he isn't there and you want to see if he's packed up and gone, you just slip a knife in and you can push the lock tongue back. It works on all our locks."

"It used to work on all the locks when they were twenty-odd years newer," I said.

"*Plus ça change, plus c'est la même chose,*" Tommy said. "And how's that for showing off my education?"

"I'm impressed," I said.

Tommy chuckled. "So am I," he said. "I wish I could go with you, but I can't. So good hunting."

I thanked him and started out of the dining room. I hadn't gone as far as the door before I was surrounded. Where I went, my friends and allies were going, too.

I gave them a warning.

"What I have in mind to do," I said, "could well turn out to be breaking and entering."

"All the more reason for having us with you," Slammer said. "For breaking and entering you are going to need lookouts."

"In case you haven't noticed," Bob said, "Slammer made the wrong marriage. Underneath all our connubial bliss she has always been a frustrated gun moll."

"Not much in the way of high adventure comes the way of a faculty wife," Slammer said. "I have me a swash-buckling type who almost never swashes."

"Be grateful I don't buckle," Bob said.

All the way across the Quad they kept up this merry

prattle. If Larry and I had been less enthusiastic about going along with it, we might have noticed that Jane Struthers was remaining silent. It was only when she broke into it with her question that we saw that she was having the shakes.

"Where?" she asked. "The dean's office?"

"No," I said. "We've done that. There's nothing there." I headed for the entry I wanted.

"Our room?" Bob said. "No need for anything sneaky. We'll let him in, won't we, Slammer?"

"If Matt prefers to break and enter," Slammer said, "let him have his fun."

"Right across the hall from you," I said. "The dorm room of the Dowling son and heir."

"And I didn't even know we'd moved into the high-rent district, though there is the Dom Perignon next door," Slammer said.

"Dowlings are big game, Matt," Bob said.

"And," I said, "killers aren't small."

"He's a dreadful child," Slammer said, "but you can't be suspecting him."

"Of murder? No. Of knowing something he shouldn't be keeping for himself? Yes."

We were into the entry and at the room door. I knocked. There was no response. The door wasn't opened. Nobody was saying "Come in." Nobody was saying "Go away" either. Nobody was saying anything. I waited a decent interval and then gave it a heavier knuckle. There was still no response.

I brought out my pocket knife and unfolded its longest blade. It wasn't quite long enough. I remembered belatedly that it had been a dinner knife we used for this purpose.

"He carries a knife," Larry said.

"An insufficient knife." Bob corrected him. He's a superannuated Boy Scout. So it follows. He's unprepared."

"Not totally unprepared," I said. "New type Boy Scout."

I brought out a credit card. It was long enough and it worked. It always does. I've heard that 'loid men are a happy lot in this era. For opening hotel room doors with intent of burglary they no longer need to carry any possibly incriminating strip of celluloid. You can't be incriminated by a credit card. Everyone carries them, the righteous and the unrighteous. Credit cards make the world go round.

I pushed the door open and as quickly shut it again.

"You girls don't want to see this," I said.

Jane turned away. Slammer stood her ground.

"Don't give us any of that," she said.

"What is it?" Bob asked.

"Murder," I said.

"We know that," Slammer said. "It's been murder all along."

"No," I said. "Now it's murder again, because I can't believe it's suicide. Anyhow it's nothing you need to see."

Larry had his own credit card out. He pushed between me and the door, worked the lock tongue back, and opening the door only wide enough for him to slip through, he went into the room and shut the door behind him. This time, though, Jane and Slammer caught a glimpse of what I'd seen in there.

Jane made a small, whimpering sound. Bob and I were just quick enough to grab her as she crumpled. She had gone limp. Between us we carried her into the Careys' room and laid her on one of the beds. Slammer took charge.

"She's only fainted," she said. "I can take care of her. You fellows go to Larry."

I still had the credit card in my hand. Bob and I went back across the hall and I went to work on the lock again. In leaving their room, Bob had shut that door behind us. Jane and Slammer had seen more than enough.

"Murder?" Bob said. "What I saw is screaming suicide."

"Maybe," I said, "but I can't believe it. It's too damned convenient. Also I think there's one missing ingredient. We'll see as soon as I get us in there."

"Gay," Bob said. "Transvestite. They're not happy types. They run heavily to suicide."

"All of which somebody had in mind when he was cooking it up," I said.

I had the door open. Larry was occupied with the body, and Bob joined him. I was leaving that for later. My mind was on the missing ingredient. I was looking for that. If I was right and it wasn't there, then I had to be right about the rest of it. This wasn't suicide. It was a murder designed to look like suicide, but the killer had slipped. His fake was only half cooked.

The body was young Rick Dowling's. In this room that looked more like the studio of a high-powered professional photographer than any undergraduate's dorm room, he was hanging by the neck from a camera boom.

As a suicide method hanging is feasible. Your man fixes his noose, fastens it to a chandelier or some other overhead fixture strong enough to take his weight, settles the noose around his neck, climbs on a stool or a chair or a table or a stepladder; then, kicking whatever out from under him, he's pulled his own trap.

It can be done and it has been done often enough, but somewhere below the dangling feet of the hanged man you are going to find that overturned chair or what have you. I was looking for that and I was finding nothing. I was trying to figure all possible alternatives. He climbs on top of some stable object—his bed, the top of his desk—and he jumps off to dangle. Considering that possibility, I concluded that it was probably unorthodox but not unfeasible.

Just by eye I did a rough calculation of the necessary geometry. There was no way it could have been made to work. I'm not an engineer for nothing. I have the requisite eye for angles, lengths, and distances. The bed, the desk top, and the windowsill all offered surfaces on which he could have stood poised for the leap into the abyss, but none of them was close enough. To reach from any of them to where the noose was fastened would have required a longer rope, and from that extra length he couldn't have achieved the fatal dangle. He would just have jumped to the floor with a rope around his neck.

The boom mechanism, on the other hand, was simple and it could have been made to order. A turn of a crank would raise or lower the heavy steel arm to which the camera would be fixed. To think that the boy stood with the noose around his neck and cranked himself up to hanging height was manifestly absurd. That would have been an effort beyond the capacity of even the most determined suicide.

And there again the distances were wrong. By the time he might have cranked the thing up to where the noose would have begun to put even the slightest pressure on his neck, his length of rope would have pulled him away from the crank handle. For taking the turn on it that would have lifted him off the floor, the handle would have been out of reach.

Larry and Bob were preoccupied with the body, and I must grant them that, apart from the boy being dead, which is a thing nobody could call insignificant, the body was arresting. It was, however, only arresting. Compared to what I was exploring, it signified little.

All those superpreppy habiliments the Dowling boy had been wearing since that time of his metamorphosis were lying scattered around the room. A couple of shirt buttons lay on the floor. Without touching it, I looked at the blue oxford button-down. I could see where the buttons had ripped off it. In some kind of frenzy the kid had torn his clothes off. In my thinking it was more likely that they had been ripped off him by somcone who wasn't taking the time for any unbuttoning.

He was hanging naked but for one item that could have been calculated to grab the attention of any observer and to keep the observer's mind off anything else there was to be seen.

All there was in the way of cover for the body's nakedness was a woman's girdle. It was that one item that had Bob riveted. Larry was a long way from ignoring it, but he was also concerned with other aspects of the corpse. He commented on the temperature of the body.

"He's cold," he said. "In this closed, hot room postmortem cooling would not have been quick. He's been dead for some time."

"Oughtn't we take him down?" Bob asked.

"No," Larry said. "We leave that for the police. We touch nothing."

"Since it's murder," I said, "we most particularly touch nothing."

"How do you make it murder?" Larry asked.

He wasn't disputing me. He was just asking.

I went through the mechanics of the thing and they followed along all the way, making each eye measurement as I pointed it out to them.

"Drugged or knocked unconscious," I said.

Larry interrupted to cut it down to knocked unconscious.

"He knew about Sooey and he knew her killer," he said. "He wasn't likely to let the guy buy him a drink."

"Find any marks on him?" Bob asked. "Wouldn't there be marks?"

"Fill a sock with sand and sap a man with it," I said. "You can put him out very nicely without leaving a mark."

"Where would anyone find sand around here?" Bob asked. "Or does he come prepared for all contingencies?"

He was asking the questions, but I could see that he had no more than half a mind for them. He couldn't take his eyes off the girdle. It had him transfixed.

"It doesn't have to be sand," Larry said. "A bar of soap in a sock is just as good if not even better."

"And everybody has soap," I said. "Everybody showers."

"Stripping him down and putting the girdle on him," Larry said. "That was a smart touch. You'd think that anyone that smart wouldn't have missed on overturning a chair and leaving it in the right position."

"He was so wrapped up in the brilliant stroke of the girdle that he let the essential thing slip his mind," I said. "A man can't think of everything. He thought of so much. Take for instance his seeing how he could use the camera boom. You knock a man out. You have him lying on the floor. You fix a noose. You put it around his neck. You've still got to hang him. Supporting his weight till you have him up high enough and holding him there while you're securing the other end of the rope? Just picture it. I'd say it's impossible to do. Even if a man had the strength for it, he couldn't possibly have that many hands. But here he had the ready-made means. He spotted it and he used it."

I ran through the whole thing for them. It was an all but effortless process. No sweat. No strain. He had the kid knocked out. He fastened the noose around the boy's neck, secured the other end of the rope to the boom arm. Then there was nothing to it but to turn the crank until he had the arm up to necessary hanging height.

"Do we call Dean Daniel or the police chief?" Larry asked. "We should be calling and now."

"Dean Danny," I said, "and across the hall. We don't want to touch anything in here, not even the phone." I turned to Bob since I was talking about using the phone in his room. At that very moment he was reaching out to touch the girdle.

"Bob," I yelled. Making a quick grab, I hauled him away from it.

"We were just saying we touch nothing," Larry said.

"Yeah," Bob mumbled.

I was remembering one game when Bob was kicked in the head and we had to lead him off the field. He seemed almost like that now. We almost had to push him out of the room and across the hall. I could understand how a spectacle of such extreme obscenity might knock any man over, but this was Bob Carey, learned Classicist. This was the guy who in the old days used to translate chunks of Suetonius for Larry and me. This was the guy who had read all that stuff on the Roman emperors—Caligula, Tiberius. How come he was going into shock?

Larry made the call. He was the best man for it. He could give it the detached, clinical observer's touch. Jane had come out of her faint. She was lying down and looking a little bluish around the mouth, but she was all right. Hearing what Larry was saying into the phone, she began crying. It was nothing hysterical. Just the tears came up in her eyes and brimmed over.

Slammer was also looking a little blue around the lips but she was holding steady.

"So peculiar for a murder," she said. "I had only a glimpse, but he was wearing a girdle, wasn't he? A woman's girdle?"

I gave her my rundown on the mechanics of the hanging. She was quick to get the point.

"This impossible skunk got himself so busy fancying the thing up that he forgot the obvious," she said.

"The first rule of crime, in fact the first rule of anything," I said, "is keep it simple. The more elaborate and complicated a thing is, the more ways it can go wrong."

Bob shook himself. It had been some sort of paralysis that had been holding him. He was pulling himself out of it. He looked like a dog coming out of the water.

"Slammer," he said. "There's something you should be doing right away. I know you'll think I'm crazy, darling, but do it."

"Sane or otherwise," Slammer said, "you know your word is my command."

Her tone was light, but there was nothing of lightness in her look. She was watching Bob and she wasn't liking what she saw. She looked worried, possibly even frightened.

He took note of her tone but he evidently missed out on her look.

"It's not a joke, kid," he said. "I want you to look. I want you to look carefully. I'd like to know before the dean or the police or anyone else gets over here and that will be almost immediately. You brought an extra girdle, I think. Is it missing?"

"Two extras," Slammer began. Then she stopped short.

After one gasping breath she spoke again. "You mean mine? On that dead child, mine?"

Something like a break into hysteria began to show in her voice.

"Just look and check on it," Bob said. "Now, dear, please."

It was now her turn to shake free of the revulsion and shock. With trembling hands she reached for a suitcase. Bob picked it up and set it on the bed for her. She lifted the lid. For my money she had no need to go further.

I can't believe that there is a woman anywhere in the world who would make that kind of a tangled mess of her packing. Any woman who did could never dress without looking like an unmade bed, and that was certainly not Slammer. She was not a fancy dresser but she always looked smooth and serene, nothing rumpled, nothing messy.

She stood for only a moment, staring at the things she had in the case and then she began pawing through it, searching with frantic and ineffectual haste. After a moment, however, she got a grip on herself. She took the things out of the case one by one and laid them aside on the bed. She said nothing until she had emptied the case. Then she spoke.

"Yes," she said. "I am missing a girdle."

"Maybe in another bag," Jane said. She had stopped crying.

Slammer went through the rest of her luggage.

"I am missing a girdle," she said again.

CHAPTER 9

The dean arrived, and he had a retinue with him. There was the police chief, this time backed up by a couple of additional cops. There was the university counsel. There was the university physician and another doctor, that one attached to the police chief. There was the great man himself, the president of the university. I had to assume that the death of a Dowling would demand that much.

Inevitably their arrival had not gone unnoticed in the Quad. By the time they reached us they had tagging along after them the most ill-assorted of all possible pairs, Ham Roberts and Culver Hoyt. There were others as well, the reunion chairman and a couple of class officers. There was also my young friend Tommy. He came in close on the heels of Ham and Culver.

Somewhat belatedly the police chief woke up to the fact that things were getting overcrowded. He set his cops up to bite it off there. He posted them at the door to the entry with orders to keep all others out.

Upstairs these extra people who had been allowed to filter in just milled around purposelessly. Only Tommy seemed to have any idea of what he was about. I could understand that. In the first place he was well aware that it had been he who had steered me to young Dowling's room. It wasn't unnatural for him to have some concern over the possibility that he might have put me in trouble. I could also imagine that he had pushed himself in with a double purpose.

You may remember that in the dining room fight it had been Tommy who had been effective in separating the combatants and imposing a cease-fire. He had been keeping an eye on Ham and Culver ever since. Seeing the two of them come together after all that time they had been keeping a distance between them, he might easily have been thinking that there could again be a need of him to keep the peace.

Erridge, of course, was back in his old role of crying murder, but this time it was different. This time I was not up against any intractable skepticism. This time the victim was Rick Dowling. It was obvious that, given the choice between informing the great Paul Dowling that his son was a suicide and bringing him the intelligence that his boy had been murdered, the latter would have to be the more welcome of the unwelcome alternatives.

Murder makes nobody happy, but no stigma attaches to being the victim of a murder. That a boy has been murdered carries no suggestion that a parent may have been doing less than well with his job of parenting.

Dean Danny pulled me aside.

"The lad was in trouble," he said. "He could have been desperate. You're certain it's murder?"

I showed him the evidence and I went through the reasoning for him. I seemed to be lifting a great burden off him. I suppose he realized that he was letting it show and felt that he had to explain why my proofs should have been so much of a relief to him.

"The boy was on drugs," he said, "and he wasn't even discreet about it. I did everything I could think of in an effort to get him straightened around, but he was an arrogant kid. He thought he was untouchable. Everybody knows how generous the Dowlings have been to us. Of course, that doesn't mean that the university is for sale, but young Rick thought we were. I could do nothing with him. I had to take it up with Paul."

"His father?"

"Yes. Paul Dowling. I must say this for Paul. He behaved well. I don't know that there are many fathers who would take a thing like that as well as he did. He recognized at once that we couldn't just let Rick stay in school. He asked only one thing of us, that instead of expelling the boy, we leave it to him to withdraw the kid. That was little enough to ask."

His account of the kid's situation cleared up the one thing I'd been having trouble with, the money angle. Even a need for supporting an expensive drug habit had not seemed enough to account for what had appeared to be a money hunger inordinate for a Dowling. I couldn't see the boy in any guise but that of a blackmailer, and for a kid who had the Dowling billions in his future I just couldn't make that kind of greed fit.

The way Dean Danny had it, Paul Dowling had come down hard on his son. For the next year or for as many more as it might take to straighten him out, Rick's old man was going to put him in a job. He was to live at home under the paternal thumb and the job would be no sinecure. He would have been working as a laborer.

Daddy had figured the whole thing out. He had even chosen the specific job. It would have been hard and dirty and sonny-boy would have been working under a hand-picked foreman.

"When he told me his plans for Rick," the dean said, "I could almost be sorry for the boy. He was putting the kid under the toughest and most brutal foreman in the works, and the man would have orders to give Rick a hard time. Paul even told me that he'd chosen a man only a few years away from retirement because a younger man might have thought ahead to the years when Rick Dowling could be expected to become a power in the company. Paul didn't want anyone who might get in some early licks at currying favor by going easy."

"That explains the kid," I said. "He wasn't about to go home to any of that. He had other ideas and he was working at financing them."

"Yes. He was over eighteen and officially that's a responsible adult, no matter how immature. Paul would have had no way of forcing him or even of controlling him except through the hold that the Dowling money might have had on him."

"Right. And he thought he'd found a way of breaking loose from the money hold. He didn't have to stay on daddy's dole. He was going to show his father. With good old Dowling enterprise he was going to make it on his own. Blackmail was going to do it for him."

Privately I was thinking that he might even have been expecting to gain his old man's approbation. He would have been demonstrating that he had the ability to make a pretty buck. In a Dowling context, of course, it would have been nothing great, but for a beginner it could have seemed enough. I could imagine that it might have impressed daddy.

I said nothing of any of that. I was listening to Dean Danny groan.

"I didn't enjoy my last session with Paul," he said. "So now I have another coming up that will be worse. On the drug problem Paul could console himself with the thought that he only had to rescue his son from the malady of the times, from being like the rest of his generation. That, of course, is a lot of crap, but there was nothing to be served by telling him so. But how do you go about telling a man that his son was a blackmailer?"

"Yes," I said. "Blackmail is something else. Dowling isn't going to be able to make himself believe that all the boys and girls are doing it."

Groaning again, the dean pulled away from it for a change of subject.

"About these murders now, Matt," he said.

"Yes, Dan?"

"This killer—Mrs. Graystock was blackmailing him. So he killed her. Rick saw enough or heard enough to know it was murder and to know who did it. Rick tried his hand at blackmailing the killer, and all he got for himself out of it was, again, murder."

"Right," I said. "Then if we fit in all the other bits and pieces, we are forced to claim this murderer for our illustrious class. I'm ready to call him Classmate Killer."

"Yes," he said. "I'm sorry."

"Why? You have nothing to apologize for. We were never your responsibility."

"I don't know how to say this," the dean began.

"Anything you have on your mind," I said.

"Hasn't it begun to look as though this classmate of yours entertains some sort of special feeling for you and Larry Dawson, either of you or both?"

"The first killing in our room," I said, "and the capsules in my bag."

"Of course, that could have been only because your room was handy and you had left your door unlocked."

"Come on, Dan! Don't pretend you don't know what

these locks are worth. Was yours the only college generation that didn't know how to open them?"

"Yes," the dean said. "We can't kid ourselves. A special
feeling."

"Larry being a medico might explain that much of it," I
said. "He could have been thinking that if anyone started
smelling murder, there would be questions about where the
barbiturates had come from. People would get busy looking at Larry Dawson, and that could have seemed a useful
diversion."

"I'm afraid the girdle knocks that idea on the head. You
can say that the room right across the hall was so handy
that it would have been inevitable that the man should
have gone there, but isn't it too much of a coincidence that
it should have been the Carey room, Mrs. Carey's girdle?"

"The nearest he could come to Larry or me in that department," I said, "since neither of us is married. Bob
Carey, Larry Dawson, and myself, he would think of us as
the inseparables. We were that."

"We've always carried on with the myth that we're one
big, happy family," the dean said. "Everyone who ever matriculated here loves everyone else who ever matriculated
here. We're all brothers in a family that never even heard
of sibling rivalry. That's our myth, but there isn't a one of
us who doesn't know better. Have you thought about this
thing from that angle, Matt? Some old grudge? Someone
who might be working off some old scores? Let's say as a
by-product of the murders."

Answering him on that, I gave it the light touch.

"We've always been considered lovable types, the three
of us," I said.

I was stalling. There was the obvious answer, Ham Roberts, but I was uncomfortable about digging up that old

story and I couldn't feel that even in having the thought I was standing on anything you could call solid ground. This old-animosity approach, after all, could cut both ways.

I didn't like Ham Roberts. I had never liked the guy, and now on renewed acquaintance I'd been finding him no less distasteful. If I had to choose among all the men back for reunion, wouldn't it be Roberts who would be my happiest choice? Dean Danny was asking me to speak out of prejudice. I wasn't prepared to do that.

He wasn't prepared to push me.

"Think about it," he said. "Talk it over with Bob and Larry. If any of you comes up with anything, let me know."

"Will do," I said.

We were doing this in Bob and Slammer's room. The police and the doctors were across the hall busying themselves with the corpse and the murder room. Larry was with them. I might have thought that Culver Hoyt, MD, should have been with them, too, but I quite forgot that he was a doctor. He was so busy being a sociologist and a detective that it might even have been that for once in his life even he was forgetting his degree and his profession.

He wasn't being specific and he wasn't giving out with any names. Tommy was right there in the room and Culver was pointedly not looking at him, but he was off and winging on his young-guttersnipe line. The Dowlings had enemies. It was the penalty people in high places have to pay. All anyone has to do is make a success in life and he quickly learns what it's like—the hatred of the Commies and the envy of the failures.

"That wonderful boy across the hall had enemies right here on campus," Culver said. He was talking directly at the dean. "That's where you have to look. Look to his fellow students who hated him because he carried the Dowling name."

The idiot was building the thing into something like a political assassination, a precursor of red revolution. He appealed to history. Hadn't the nihilists murdered Russian Grand Dukes? Didn't we all know what it finally came to in Russia? It would have been boring and possibly even funny if young Tommy hadn't been there to hear it. As it was, nobody could laugh. It was too nasty.

Dean Daniel tried to turn him off. He spoke up for the soundness of the young, but that kind of talk has never made any impression on the Culver Hoyts. It just spurs them on to new extremes of ugly absurdity.

The dean was a good man, but he had his limits. Or possibly he had been through this kind of nonsense too many times before. He knew a lost cause when he saw one. He turned his back on it and moved away to talk to Jane Struthers. He told her that he had been on to Amanda Graystock's attorney. According to the lawyer, Sooey had been alone in the world with no living relatives.

"He tells me," the dean said, "that in her will she left a bequest to the university in memory of George Graystock and that her personal belongings and the residue of her estate are to go in equal parts to her two friends, Alberta Smith and Jane Struthers."

Jane, who had long since pulled herself together and dried her tears, now had a new flow to mop away.

"Oh, dear," she said. "I never thought."

She sounded as though she might almost be afraid that someone would think it was she who had killed Sooey since she would be inheriting this pittance.

"The lawyer says he knows you."

"Yes, I met him through Amanda. I've come to know him well."

"Everything will have to be held for the legal formalities," the dean said. "Appraisals for the tax people and all that stuff."

"I know," Jane said. "I've been through it with my husband's estate. There's no hurry. It doesn't matter."

"He suggested that I turn over her suitcase and her purse to you. I'll get them over here for you. You'll have them before you leave, but I've been carrying her keys around."

I remembered how it had been when we first found Sooey's body. I had looked for her purse then, trying to make sense of the barbiturate bottle. She hadn't had it with her. Evidently she had left it back in her room and it had been taken to the dean's office with her suitcase. I had to assume that the dean had inspected the contents of the purse. Obviously he had found her keys there.

He fished them out of his pocket and he was holding them in his hand. I saw the thing that had been haunting me, the one small, solid item I'd been trying to remember. There was that one key that was not attached to the ring in the ordinary way. It was fastened with a twist of tape. It was a key that was not designed to go on a ring. It lacked the small hole in the butt end through which a ring could go.

"Mrs. Smith is still too shaken," Dean Danny said.

"I can understand that. I'm not too steady myself," Jane said, "and I haven't been through what she has."

She took the keys from Mulligan's hand and held them for a moment or two. She was still on the bed, although now she was sitting up. She seemed to be looking for something.

I had moved in close. Anything to keep those keys in

sight. I wanted them. I hadn't even the first idea of how I could get my hands on them.

"Something you want, Jane?" I asked. "Anything I can get you?"

"My purse," she said. "I had it here somewhere."

It was across the room, sitting on top of a chest of drawers. The chest stood alongside the door to the hall.

"I see it," I said, reaching for the keys. "Let me stow those for you."

Quickly—I could say even eagerly—she pushed the key ring into my hand.

"Would you?" she said. "You are a dear."

She wasn't happy with her role of heiress. It had come too close upon her grief for her dead friend. She was not yet ready to think about it and she didn't want to be reminded.

I needed the keys. It was all very well that the authorities were now recognizing murder for what it was. Their recognition was still limited to the one murder, this Rick Dowling killing. I knew what tack they were going to take on that. The mayor and the police chief would be taking the undergraduate-devil line.

I had seen enough of this pair, and I could remember their predecessors. Even back then nothing had gone wrong in the town that didn't produce the automatic assumption. It's them young devils again. They were going to need to have forced on them the recognition that the two killings were linked. They were even still to be convinced that Sooey's death had been murder.

I had the keys. I moved to the door. I made the requisite stop at the chest of drawers. Opening her purse, I did what I hoped would be a good fake of dropping the keys into it.

With a great show of care I closed the handbag. I still had the keys hidden in my hand.

I was itching to be out the door but I was afraid I mightn't be able to get away with too abrupt an exit. I hung on for a while, lounging in the doorway. After a few minutes I thought of something. Putting my hand in my pocket served a double purpose. I got the keys out of my hand and I brought out my cigarettes. I fished one out of the pack and stuck it between my lips. I brought out my lighter and had the flame only an inch away from the tip of the cigarette when I switched into a considerate-smoker act. I was thinking better of it. The room was too full of people. It was no place for a smoke. With the unlit cigarette between my lips I stepped out of the room.

There would still be the cops down at the entry door. I was going to have to get past them. I waited with my cigarette until I had reached them. There I lit up. I was hoping it looked natural, a man just stepping out into the Quad for a smoke. I needn't have bothered. They had no interest in me. Their orders were to keep people out. Nobody had told them to keep people in.

I could have wished that classmates and their wives out in the Quad had been similarly lacking in interest. They crowded around me. They wanted to know what was happening. I fobbed them off with the quickest answer I could think up.

"Something to do with an undergraduate," I said. "I really don't know . . ."

It was only part of a lie. I didn't know. I didn't have to tell them that I was on my way to find out.

There was the key not made to fit on a key ring. I knew of only one kind of lock that had such a key. It lacked the little hole the ring could go through, but where the hole would have been in any other kind of key it had a number hammered into the metal. The number was 14A.

It was the key to a luggage locker, locker No. 14A. I knew where I could go in town to find luggage lockers. I hadn't the first doubt of being on target.

I did have two things bothering me. Since Sooey hadn't brought the thing her killer wanted to the dorm and she had been carrying this luggage locker key, it had to be that she had taken the precaution of leaving the thing locked away in Locker 14A. It didn't necessarily follow, though, that she had brought the thing to town with her. Locker 14A might not be here. It could be in any town anywhere.

I was telling myself that I was spooking me unnecessarily. It would be here in town, just across the street from the front campus. It would be in the bus station. If Sooey had stowed it somewhere before she came to reunion, certainly she wouldn't have been carrying the key with her. She would have left the key at home. Also, since she must have been planning to use it, she would have needed to have it somewhere reasonably close to hand.

I suppose it was some feeling that I was getting too enthusiastically hopeful that had me thinking up things to tamp down my expectations. I had her key ring and there was on it only one key that could possibly be a luggage key. I worked up for myself the picture of finding in the locker a locked suitcase and no key for opening it.

Could even Sooey have been so silly that she would bring a locked case and not the key to open it? I told myself that if there were another locked case, it would be one of a set with one key fitting the locks of all the pieces. I worked at convincing myself that it had to be that way. I had thought of jumping into the Porsche and doing the quick roll over to the bus station, but I'd decided against it.

I'd been along that street that bordered the campus and I knew it was solid with parked cars. Taking Baby, I would have been ever and a day finding a place to park her. I could do it quicker on foot.

I was racing along even while I was telling myself that there wasn't all that need for hurry. It was there, whatever it was. It was locked away. I was holding the key. It wouldn't go away. But then again I was holding the key and I had no right to be holding it. There was a reason for haste. I couldn't go on forever before I got that key ring into Jane's handbag. It was either that or come up with pay dirt.

As I approached the bus station, I could see that it was dark. I looked at my watch. I didn't know when I had last thought of the time. It was well past midnight. The last buses would have come and gone. Was I going to find the bus station locked? I wasn't ready to break the bus station door down, and I was wondering whether I could hope for a lock that would respond to a credit card.

By then I was taking it on the run. I hit the bus station and I tried the door. It wasn't locked. I should have known it wouldn't be. People with belongings in the luggage lockers could hardly be given less than twenty-four-hour access.

It was dark in there. I could just make out the locked grille down over the ticket window and at the back of the place the big bulk that would be the battery of luggage lockers.

I looked for 14A. I had to do it by the little flame of my cigarette lighter. There was no 14A. There were no A numbers at all. Unused lockers had their keys in the heyholes. They were like the one I was holding only in that they, too, were without the hole for fitting on a key ring. Otherwise they were of a different size and a different shape.

I went out of the bus station and I was dragging. Silly, soft-headed Sooey had done what I'd been telling myself she couldn't have possibly done. The key would fit a locker in another place, another town, anywhere. I was no sooner out in the street, however, that I remembered something and I picked up.

Maybe it was the alliteration that brought it in for me. Silly, soft-headed, sentimental Sooey—of course she hadn't come by bus. She had come the way we always used to come and go back when we were young. The bus company ran a good schedule and train service had gone to hell. So now, long after everyone else had given up on the railroad where trains were few, far between, and always fantastically behind schedule, Sooey had come by train.

I crossed the street and dove into the campus. I was taking the shortcut, across campus to the train station. All over the campus reunions were going full tilt. All the walks were filled with characters adrift from one reunion to the next. Everyone else was strolling. Only Erridge was taking it on the run. All the way through the campus I was followed by derisive cheers. I kept catching fragments of cracks about midnight joggers.

Once I was clear of the campus, however, I was away from all that. I was running down a gravel path, running in the dark and the quiet. The sounds of campus revelry reached me only from a distance. I was away from the people and the shouting and the music.

Unlike the bus station, the train depot wasn't dark. The light in the waiting room was dim, but there was a light. Through the windows, as I approached it, I could see what I wanted to see. The row of luggage lockers was still there.

Nothing had changed. Nothing had been moved. It was exactly as I remembered it from the late nights in the old days. Even then there had been no trains after midnight, not until the milk train would come in along about daybreak. After that last train of the night they would mop down the waiting room floor. The place had its nighttime smell of detergent and ammonia. The smell used to hang on in that waiting room and it would still be there, even if only faintly, when the milk train would bring us back from the city after a big night on the town. Things were so much unchanged that even the old smell was there, but this night freshly strong and acrid.

It used to be said that there were guys who in the late-night hours took their girls to the waiting room bench. I wondered if there would be any who were doing that now, and I thought not. The days of open dorm room doors and one foot on the floor were long gone. I doubted that anyone had used the station that way even back in our day. It was probably just one of the myths. The old place had always been full of myths.

I tore into the waiting room and headed straight for the lockers. I was okay. The lockers were in two banks. One had the A numbers and the other the Bs. Locating 14A, I rammed the key into the lock and swung the door open.

At first sight I thought the damn thing was empty. As I've told you, that waiting room light was dim and I had been expecting a suitcase or at least something like a dispatch case. There was just nothing bulking up inside that dimly lit box. Dim as it was, I needed no more light for seeing that much.

Then I saw it. It lay on the floor of the locker and it didn't bulk up at all. It was just a flat manila envelope. It was pushed back deep in the locker. I reached in for it. My fingers had not quite touched it when the arm came swinging in past my ear and the forearm slammed back hard against my throat. I was being dragged backward, away from the envelope and away from the locker.

I tried to fight it. I was struggling to break the grip, but it was strangling me, and in a fight strangulation does nothing for a man's competence. I was in trouble. If I didn't know all the dirty-fighting methods for breaking that hold, I knew most of them. None were any good to me that night.

I couldn't get my feet planted for the solid footing I would have needed for making any move I knew. The floor was slick, still wet from the mopping. The tiles were slippery with unrinsed detergent.

Everything I tried just put me in worse shape. I was slipping and sliding and with each slip and each slide I was being brought more firmly under control. I couldn't kid myself that control would be all that was wanted. It wasn't the first time I'd had a close look at death, but this time it was so close that I could taste it and smell it.

However futilely, I kept flailing around. Most of it, of course, was the desperate effort to break the grip but even then some little part of it was trying to twist around to see who it was that had it on me. Don't ask me why, if this was to be it, I should have had so great a curiosity to know who was killing me. This I remember clearly. I did want to know.

My sight was blurring and going dim. Some of that was the sweat running down into my eyes, but no little of it was strangulation. I was making one last great effort with every certainty that it would be my last. I knew I didn't have another one in me. To my astonishment I seemed to be doing better with it than I had with any of my earlier and stronger efforts. That was contrary to all expectations. I was even managing to get twisted around to where I could see. I saw big young Tommy.

My head swam. How much of that was strangulation and how much shock and bewilderment I'll never know. Culver Hoyt had all but fingered the kid, but that had never made any sense. Culver's notions about Tommy and the Dowlings had seemed stupid enough, but Sooey? What could she have had that could have mattered in any way to this boy who was young enough to have been her son? Another possibility went shooting through my head. I was the one who had been looking for the Dowling boy and making a big thing of it. Could Tommy now be thinking that what I had been after was murder and that I had sucked him into helping me do it?

He could have been thinking that, but would he in turn be wanting to kill me for what he thought I had done? Wouldn't he settle for grabbing me and holding me for the police?

I had broken loose and was shaking the fog out of my head when I came around far enough to see the whole of it. Tommy had his big hands not on me but on old Neil Neecey. With one mammoth paw he'd dragged Culver off me. With the other he was even now in the act of clipping Culver on the chin. Culver went down to the slippery floor and Tommy went down astride him.

"I've got him under control," Tommy said. "If you want to call the cops, there's the pay phone you can use. Better get the campus switchboard to ring Rick Dowling's room. Just about every cop the town's got is over there making an ass of himself."

"Mind holding him just a little longer?" I said.

"My pleasure. It's the guttersnipe in me. You know

when he was going on and on about what a great little gentleman Rick Dowling was, he had already killed him."

I knew. It was of a piece with his valiant defense of Sooey's good name. Neil Neecey all the way. Speak nothing but good of his victims.

I hauled the envelope out of the locker and on the way across the waiting room to the phone I ripped it open. It had only one thing in it. It was a marriage license fully executed—Amanda and Culver in July twenty years back. That would have been a few weeks after we graduated.

I looked at Culver where Tommy had him pinned to the floor. He had made enough of a recovery from the clip to be flailing about, but it was doing him no good. Tommy had him too much outweighed and too much outmuscled. Culver saw me with the paper in my hand and he lay still.

"Look, men," he said. "Look. We were drunk. It never came to anything. I just about forgot it ever happened."

"Never even came to mind when you were at the altar with Florence?"

"Yes, of course, but you must see I couldn't start a divorce then."

"How about just a little earlier when you were thinking of asking Florence to marry you?"

"I couldn't. I would have lost Florence. She's a Catholic. She'd never have married a divorced man, her father would never have allowed it. I would have lost everything, ruined my whole life, and over something that had never been anything."

"A woman and a boy are dead," I said. "That's something that is something, old buddy."

"Blackmailers," Culver said. "Both of them, low-down contemptible blackmailers."

The tone he used in saying the word was too much the

tone he was always using for "guttersnipe." It woke unfortunate echoes.

"She never married Graystock," I said.

"Yes. I was stupid. Should a man pay with his whole life for being stupid? Look, fellows. Just burn the damn thing and that's it. The whole mess stays unsolved. The damage that's been done has been done. Do you need more? To ruin me? To kill Florence? Because this will kill her. I did it for her. Can't you see that I did it for her?"

Tommy looked at me and I looked at him. We didn't have to say anything to each other.

"Do we need more?" I said. "We don't need a two-time killer back to putting women on the operating table. A killer surgeon? We need that?"

"Look," he said. "I'll retire from practice. I won't operate any more."

"Culver," I said. "You're retired right now."

I dropped my dime in the pay phone and I called the police.

You may be interested. Florence Hoyt didn't die. She was embarrassed. The process of getting a divorce from a man to whom she had never been legally married must have been a humiliation, and there was also the annulment from her church.

The dean's idea about someone settling an old score by throwing suspicion my way may not have been too far off the mark. It wouldn't have been my way, however, but Larry's. Remember all that help the dimwit had taken from Larry in our college days. That had been something he had never been able to forgive. I guess it had always eaten at him that Larry was a better brain and a better man than he could ever have hoped to be. Piled onto that there had been Larry's contempt. He couldn't have been unaware of that. If you ever want an enemy, look for some guy who once bruised his ego by going to you for help.

We none of us—Alberta, Jane, Slammer, Bob, Larry, or myself—will ever believe that Sooey really blackmailed the stupid louse. She had been too considerate of him. When Graystock wanted to marry her, she could all too easily have rid herself of the Culver impediment. She'd had grounds enough many times over. They hadn't been near each other for all those years, and the man was a bigamist.

She hadn't done it. Instead she had lived with Graystock without marrying him. That she had done out of consideration for Culver Hoyt. Sooey was not a woman who would mess up any man's life. So blackmail?

Over the years she had been doing Culver a great service, and now she was on the edge of being in need. Culver was loaded, and who can say that she shouldn't have felt that he owed her something? We think she did no more than ask him for help and, being Culver Hoyt, he overreacted.

The evidence tucked away in the luggage locker?

She didn't know whether he would remember. She might have needed it to refresh his memory, but she hadn't wanted to make trouble for him. She wasn't going to bring it to the dorm just in case somehow someone might see it.

I know you think we're leaning over backward to see her in the best possible light. Rose-colored glasses and all that.

But if you knew Sooey like we knew Sooey . . .